USA *Today* Bestselling Author

TRILINA PUCCI

synopsis

IMAGINE DATING A GUY FOR SIX MONTHS, AND THEN ONE NIGHT, YOU MAKE HIM DINNER SO YOU CAN SAY I LOVE YOU FOR THE FIRST TIME.

ROMANTIC, RIGHT?

NO, BECAUSE WHEN YOU DRESS UP AS DESSERT, HE TELLS YOU HE'D RATHER BE A PARTY OF ONE. LEAVING YOU TO CRY IN YOUR WHIPPED CREAM BOOBS, DRINK A BOTTLE OF TEQUILA, AND DEBATE ON CUTTING BANGS.

ROCK BOTTOM, YOU SAY?

WRONG, AGAIN.

NOT ONLY DOES HE BREAK UP WITH YOU, BUT HE SHOWS UP TO THE VACATION YOU'D PLANNED WITH YOUR FRIENDS.

SO NOW, HERE I SIT WITH MY EX, DJ DOUCHEBAG, AND HIS NEW GIRLFRIEND IN PARADISE... DID I MENTION SHE DOESN'T WEAR MAKEUP AND SPEAKS THREE LANGUAGES?

I DON'T WANT HIM BACK, BUT I ALSO DON'T WANT TO LOOK LIKE THE BEFORE TO THEIR PERFECT AFTER.

AND THAT MEANS DESPERATE TIMES CALL FOR A DIRTY DISTRACTION. A WAY TO KEEP MY MIND OFF EVERYTHING. AND THE UNIVERSE SAYS THERE'S ONLY ONE WAY TO DO THAT...

TJ AND NATE.

SO, I GUESS THAT MEANS THERE ARE ACTUALLY *THREE WAYS* TO MEND MY BROKEN HEART.

playlist

1. Flowers—Miley Cyrus
2. Buzzkill Baby—Mckenna Grace
3. Everybody Talks—Neon Trees
4. greedy—Tate McRae
5. Nuthin' But A "G" Thang—Dr. Dre & Snoop Dogg
6. Good as Hell—Lizzo
7. Mr. Brightside—The Killers
8. Selfish—Justin Timberlake
9. (I've Had) The Time of My Life—Bill Medley & Jennifer Warnes
10. TEXAS HOLD 'EM—Beyoncé
11. Not My Fault—Reneé Rapp & Megan Thee Stallion
12. yes, and?—Ariana Grande
13. Don't Start Now—Dua Lipa
14. Gin and Juice—Snoop Dogg
15. Lil Boo Thang—Paul Russell
16. Cuffing Season—Farizki

dedication

To all my exes.

Thanks for sucking.
I could've never written elite revenge without you.

dear reader,

I wrote this book with the intention of giving an "every woman" experience. That means the heroine isn't described. I did this on purpose. To allow anyone reading the chance to picture themselves or someone who looks like them. I strived to keep her as vague as possible. So enjoy, because this one's for you and you and you and YOU!

Xoxoxo, Trilina

prologue

. . .

"Her boobs are basically a Winnie the Pooh kink."

FaceTime answers

"Is this too much...for the moment? Be honest."

I move backward away from my screen so my friends can really take me in, in all my sexy glory, wearing whipped cream boobs, edible panties, and the highest heels I own.

"Oh my god," Samantha breathes out, her mouth falling open as Eleanor starts a slow clap.

I can't help but smile, bouncing on the balls of my feet.

"I know it's crazy, but 'I love you' deserves a moment." I hold up the cherry pinched between my fingers. "It's the cherry on top, right? Or am I insane? Tell me now because he's going to be here in like twenty minutes."

Eleanor smiles ear to ear. "Bitch, there is nothing more romantic than going full *Varsity Blues* to say I love you. You are a moment. Ajax's gonna lose his mind, Mills."

My teeth find my lip because the smile I'm wearing is

burning my cheeks. I know standing half-naked in my boyfriend's apartment, ready to surprise him with, well, me, is wild. But sue me, I like a grand gesture.

Samantha nods. "You literally look ravishing, Millie. A damn snack." She winks, being cheeky. "Plus, years from now, your kids will love hearing this story. Side note... how the hell did you get the Reddi-wip to stay?"

Eleanor cuts in, "You have to add honey first. Her boobs are basically a Winnie the Pooh kink."

I laugh as I make my way back to my phone and bring it to my face, but before I can say anything, I hear the lock to his apartment turn.

"Oh shit, he's here. Love you, bye."

My phone lands on the couch as I toss my hair behind my shoulders before placing a hand on my hip and posing in the only pair of red-bottom shoes I own.

"Surprise," I purr before licking my glossy lips.

Except the world slows, and my eyes start to blink as if they're trying to make sense of what I'm seeing. *Oh my god.*

I scramble an arm across the whipped cream to hide my boobs. Except it glides right over me, too quickly, making me lose my balance. And I fall—the entire six inches I was sitting pretty on a second ago.

Right into my boyfriend and his *guest*.

Because while *I love you* hung on the tip of my tongue, his was just down someone else's fucking throat.

one

· · ·

"When did you start saving yourself for Christ?"

millie

My vanilla Aviator Nation hoodie scrunches closed around my face as I tug hard on the strings. I grumble, feeling the bounce of the plane's wheels on the runway.

"Remind me why I said yes to this?"

Eleanor, my best friend, shifts in her posh leather seat to stare at me before she whooshes out a contemplative breath, pausing before saying, "Your face looks like a butthole." I narrow my eyes, making her lips press together before she continues. "Okay, I have two possible answers, but before I choose which, do you need *big sister* energy or *best friend* energy?"

I'm considering my options while still holding the strings before my answer's gritted between my teeth.

"What's the difference?"

She grins, shifting even more so her back is completely facing the aisle.

"Big sisters have zero tact and always tell the truth-truth; best friends can exist in the gray."

I purse my lips, wiggling them back and forth before I decide.

"I'm thinking bestie energy." My bottom lip protrudes just a bit before I add, "After all, there's a considerable chance that I'm still a fragile little baby dandelion."

Elle taps my nose and winks, keeping her voice gentle.

"You're here because it's the week leading up to Valentine's Day. And being that you're my soulmate and quite possibly my fiancé's other best friend, it's a no-brainer that we would want you to celebrate the season of love in paradise together with us and the Tweedles. And that'll be a fun reunion too. You haven't really hung out since Vegas."

My shoulders jostle slightly with a silent laugh over the nickname given to her fiancé's two best friends and teammates, Nate and TJ.

I think it's *the Tweedles* because they're practically inseparable. Although, I secretly think of them as Tweedle *big dick* (gray sweats are my scientific proof) and Tweedle *thigh tats*.

"Be-tee-dubs, it was hella cool of you to let them stay in your suite. Maybe you guys can have late-night pillow fights or something?"

I want to laugh at the *or something* part. I do. Except the only reason TJ and Nate have a fancy room is because my boyfriend cheated on me, in front of me, leaving me a lonely, miserable *Bridgerton* spinster with no prospects for our Valentine's Day vacay. I don't even have a gossip column to roast them in.

"Sorrows. Sorrows. Prayers for my dignity," I whisper to myself.

Eleanor rubs my arm as I drop my hands from the strings of my hoodie before un-scrunching it off my head, and holding up a finger to shut her up because I can already see a joke on the tip of her tongue.

"Elle, I can't believe I'm here…not Hawaii, but back in the place where no matter how much I want to be the girl in a rom-com who's about to accidentally bump into '*the one*,' I'm actually the '*tired of dating, always chooses assholes, and wallows in self-pity*' main character in my real life."

"Dating sucks," she commiserates.

But I huff, "Guys suck."

She chuckles. "If it makes you feel better, when Crew and I broke up, I tried to manifest witnessing a crime so I could rat out a cartel and disappear courtesy of the government."

I groan again, hating everything.

Eleanor raises a brow, gauging me before I semi-shrug and say what I should've said to start with.

"I think I need the swift kick in the ass. It's time. Don't hold back. Remind me why I really came. Just say it."

She nods and claps her hands together as I give my face some sobering taps.

"Okay…" Her hands land on my shoulders. "You came because your boyfriend showed up at his house with some rando girl. About to fuck her. After lying to you for months. And then had the nerve to ask you to pause the love talk in favor of a threesome."

I quickly cover my face before I hide in my own lap as she continues.

"And ever since, you've been wallowing in the same pajamas, and possibly skipping out on brushing your teeth, while swearing off men forever in favor of owning cats." She pats my back. "Even though pussy's never been yo' thang—"

"I hate myself," I mumble.

"Mills, if you'd stayed home, you'd be force-feeding yourself enough chocolate to become diabetic and probably spiraling over my Instagram pics since we planned this trip together. Now, take some fucking ownership of your life, and stop being a loser in Hawaii. DJ douchebag has stolen enough of your shine. The sad girl aesthetic has expired, hoe. It's time for bad bitch o'clock."

As if on cue, the alarm on my phone chimes, making Elle's laugh wrap around her words.

"See? It's time."

I sit up, rolling my eyes. "That's my birth control alarm."

"Mills, don't disrespect the universe. It's hella rude. Now, get up and grab your shit, and let's head straight to the beach."

I look at her begrudgingly before stomping my feet a million times quickly, then laughing.

"Finnneeee," I draw out. "But only because the alternative is spiraling into another spiral. I might as well be sun-kissed while wallowing in my misery. Right?"

She's grinning before making me shimmy.

"You just need a week of bad ideas and too much liquor to make it out aliving and thriving, baby."

The smile hidden before is now starting to bloom. But before I can rebuke this tiny demon of happiness taking over my body, the delicious scent of man washes over us.

And by *man*, I mean a Tweedle...specifically, TJ-fucking-Knox.

Speaking of bad ideas.

He's facing us, reaching above his head, only kind of,

because he's so tall nothing's really above his head. TJ grabs some luggage from the overhead compartment. His shirt lifted just enough to expose his happy trail and that delectable Adonis belt. Also known as the v, for *very* sexy.

God, he's so fucking hot.

It should be illegal to be as good-looking as he is *and* have a good personality. No, that's a lie. What's really illegal is to have panty-dropping green eyes, a twelve-pack, perfect teeth, and enough of a beard that I know it would leave my thighs red. All while he says shit like "darlin'" with his barely-there Southern drawl.

He's like Travis Kelce and Matthew McConaughey's love child.

A six-foot-five golden retriever with a knack for making me blush.

Damn, if only I weren't heartbroken and regretting my life choices, I could consider those pillow fights and the *or something.*

Even though he's more like a taboo novel than a rom-com, considering he likes to tag team women with the guy he's tossing a black duffle to.

Nate cracks his neck, catching it with one hand before laughing, deep and rich, at something TJ says.

What he said, I have no idea. Because Nate's inched closer to us. Actually, his glorious thighs have come closer. God, I love when guys slut out their legs. Especially when they're like Nate's, covered in tattoos, leaving very little of his olive-colored skin showing.

His eyes connect with mine as I'm sexualizing him, just as he licks his lips.

Hey, roomie. Oh my god. I almost break my neck with the speed at which I look away. Because he's the kind of guy...no, it's not his attitude—it's his eyes. Illicitly sexy,

9

brown bedroom ones. Like two pools of rich chocolate making me want to swim in all my dirty thoughts.

He's a guy who never says much but every-freaking-thing all at once.

With just a look.

And I swear just now, it was, "Get naked." Or maybe that's wishful thinking. Yeah, I'm definitely projecting.

At that thought, my eyes dart over to Eleanor's, who's smirking at me like she knows what I'm thinking.

So, I roll my eyes. *Because she does.*

Still, I look past her again at Nate's waistband, not daring to look any lower but really, really wanting to. I mean, it's basically in my face, so it's not my fault if my eyes just go, *whoops.*

Jesus, I'm so horny it's actually disgusting. And honestly, I blame Mars for being in my fifth house—she's a *sloot.*

"Hey now," Eleanor whispers, making me jerk back from my dirty thoughts. She leans in so close, so fast, that I hit my head on the plane window.

"Fuck me."

"Exactly," she whispers. "You're thinking what I'm thinking." I shake my head, knowing exactly what she's about to say before she ticks her eyes toward the aisle and mouths, *Rebound?*

"Ewww," I hiss, grinning and covering her mouth with my hand before I push her back to her side.

She rolls her eyes before pulling my hand away as we try to act cool as Nate follows TJ down the aisle.

"What's ewww?" she pushes back, enjoying herself too much. "The fact that they're actually single?" I sneer, but she winks. "If you're not ready for a new and much-improved boyfriend, then don't choose. Do them both.

They don't date the girls they share, so your heart's safe, princess."

"I hate you." I grin, wiping her gloss off my palm. "First off, I'm in emotional turmoil. Heartbroken."

She chuckles. "Liar. You're embarrassed and licking your wounds."

"Tomato, Potato...or whatever that saying is. Second, you've also literally been there, done that. So, there's no way I would ever hook up with TJ." I hold up a finger to shut her up. "Or Nate. No fucking way. My lady of the night is on strike, forever. She's untrustworthy. Can't risk another bad decision. Let alone two."

She shoves my shoulder, shaking her head.

"When did you start saving yourself for Christ? Or travel back to the 1800s. Show an ankle already, Duchess. Jesus, it was once, loser...think of it as a Yelp review. Five stars. Ten out of ten recommend that spit roast. Plus, you never know what can happen. It's late at night...the room is dark. There's R&B playing in the background."

My hoodie finds its way back over my head before I put my sunglasses on, ignoring her.

"What is wrong with you?" I chuckle because I can't help it. "You're high. Just because I'm letting them stay with me doesn't mean R&B will suddenly start playing. They have their own room. On the other side of the suite. I'm sure they'll turn it into a brothel."

Eleanor laughs and rises from her seat, making room for me to do the same.

"All I'm saying is—"

I cut her off. "No. No. You can say less. Literally."

She laughs and sticks out her tongue before looking ahead, smiling at her guy, Crew, as he lifts her bag and gives her an air smooch.

Yuck. Love.

I look inside the overhead compartment for mine, but Crew cuts off my thought as he deplanes, yelling over his shoulder.

"The boys got you, Mills."

I don't even get to say thanks before Eleanor bumps my shoulder.

"Yeah, Mills, the boys *got* you."

I huff a laugh as we walk down the aisle. "You're a foul whore. Eyes forward."

We're still chuckling as we exit the plane to a perfect cloudless state of blue in the sky. The kind of color that could only be named bliss. It's that beautiful.

Holy shit.

I take a deep breath, appreciating the crisp air as we descend the stairs. We're greeted by attendants at the bottom with "Aloha," so I dip my head as a gorgeous, vibrant lei is placed around my neck.

This is magical.

"Thank you," I breathe, lifting my face toward the sun, letting my hood fall off my head so I can bask.

This is exactly what I need. Not hot dogs flying at my face or a week of wondering if I'm catching an STD. *Just this.*

A week of nature's spiritual medicine to realign my chakras and heal me, because Hawaii is transformational.

This is my *Eat Pray Love.*

Absolutely nothing could go wrong here.

two

. . .

"You're killing me, Smalls."

millie

Before I fall into a full-on trance and commit myself to the land, I hear "Mills" yelled from the Jeeps that are waiting for us.

I open my eyes to see Nate waving me over as his giant frame hangs out.

"Come on, you're with us."

You know what else could be transformational? There you go again, Venus.

I smile at the horny thought before seeing Eleanor already waving bye as Crew peels out.

Of course, she left me.

Her definition of life wingman is to shove me out of the plane into the only cure she believes in for heart-break...*dick.*

Or, in this case, *dicks.*

The Tweedles' Jeep roars to life, so I skip-jog toward

the car, watching Nate as he reaches his muscular arm over the outside of the car to open my door.

God bless the world of professional athletes. Specifically, football players because only arms like that exist in the NFL.

"Thanks," I rush out, climbing in quickly and getting a wink from TJ in the mirror.

I grin, trying not to blush, turning my head toward the scenery. Funny enough, I did read once that flirting is good for you, so who am I to deny myself.

It's like dirty chicken soup for the horny soul.

"Hey," TJ laughs. "We gotta stop meeting like this." My brows furrow as I look back at him, confused, but he adds, "This is like the last time we hung out, except instead of taking you from the hotel to the airport, we're delivering you from the airport to the hotel."

I chuckle, nodding, remembering how fun and *very flirty* that thirty-minute drive was.

"I suppose I should start tipping you now. Since you're my official Uber driver."

TJ's shoulders lift with a small laugh as he reverses with one hand on the wheel, looking back over his shoulder and teasing, "Twenty percent or get out."

"Shit. I'm light on cash. How about two queen beds and an infinity pool?"

My lips press together as he chuckles because I'm trying to ignore how fucking hot it is when guys drive like that.

I turn my head, looking around for my seat belt, and let out a quiet laugh.

Nate runs his hand through his already tousled hair. "Hey, speaking of the room, you dodged a bullet with that DJ."

My brows shoot up, body frozen as TJ coughs out, "Ixnay on the ouchebag-day."

He's shaking his head without any subtlety or stealthiness.

Son of a bitch.

"Are you kidding me?" I shout, smacking the tops of the seats as I lunge forward.

"Seat belt," they simultaneously bark as the brakes hit.

I gripe back, falling a little forward, "She told you—" I'm ready to murder my best friend. "Eleanor told you all my business, didn't she?"

This is why your best friend isn't allowed to have other best friends. *Leaks.*

If I let myself think about all the ways I am completely humiliated right now, I would throw myself out of this car. It's bad enough Eleanor and Goddess above know. But not the Tweedles.

Hot guys don't get to know you at your worst. I've basically admitted that I shit and fart. This makes me too real, and now even the fantasy that they'd fuck me is ruined.

Jesus...they know about *the*...and *the*...oh god, the fucking whipped cream. Screw throwing myself out—I'm running Eleanor over.

Neither answers. TJ and Nate just turn around and stare at me. Nate raises a brow as TJ looks down at my lap and then back to my eyes, giving me a smirk.

"You're killing me, Smalls."

Nate lifts his chin. "Seat belt, Scrappy Doo."

I let out a groan, scooting back into my seat and clicking the damn belt closed. As I open my mouth to explain away my embarrassment, TJ clears his throat, grabbing my eyes in the mirror.

"Your girl didn't go into detail. She just said that dick did you hella dirty."

Thank god she didn't give the details. I was one step away from lighting a candle in her memory.

Nate crosses his arms behind his head, yelling his words as the car speeds up down the tree-lined road.

"If you want us to fuck him up, we will. I never liked that guy. He played too many Drake songs at the club. Usher, I could understand, but Drake? Nah, that's a red flag. You're better off."

I nod my head, laughing internally at my life.

"You guys are sweet to offer permanent relocation of his jaw," I shout.

The air whips by as I lay my head back against the seat, relishing the scent of vacation. "But that asshat is long gone. And *never* to be seen again."

Thank. Fucking. God.

three

. . .

"I said Eat Pray Love but I got Forgetting
Sarah Marshall."

millie

"What do you mean there's no reservation in my name?"

It's the second time I've asked that question. And the third time the Four Seasons front desk clerk has repeated his answer.

"As I stated, Miss... I do not show a reservation for Millicent Dwyer."

My mouth drops open and then shuts before I speak because I feel like I'm hallucinating or have suddenly found myself on one of those doctor shows where I think I'm saying real words, but what's coming out isn't making any sense.

How doesn't he understand that I, in fact, have a room because I have a fucking confirmation number. My head shifts over to Nate and TJ, who have already found snacks...some blondies and two brunettes.

"See...sir," I whisper, leaning over the counter for

privacy. "I feel like the words you're saying are different from the ones I'm hearing. I heard *no reservation*...but that's impossible because I have a confirmation number. Please, I'd just like to check in."

I spin my phone around with the email from the hotel.

His brows furrow, and I'm sure they match mine before he looks down at his computer and then back to me, still confused, before he looks down again, pressing more keys that seem to be getting us nowhere.

Ten minutes ago, I walked inside this splendor, a hotel with seemingly no walls and all-white marble floors. Pristine vibes. I was ready to relax and maybe even pay an exorbitant amount of money to get a rubdown by a waterfall.

I was already imagining my room and how I was going to run inside and jump directly onto the bed like I was a character in a movie who got a free suite upgrade.

Dear Universe, shit luck with dudes is one thing...but now the Four Seasons? You're foul for this.

"All good?" comes from a few feet beside me, so I turn my head, smiling weakly at Nate and TJ before the desk clerk speaks up again.

"I apologize. It looks as if this reservation is under a different name."

"Oh." My voice is too excited, but the relief flooding my body won't be ignored. "Sorry, I should've said Millie. Nobody calls me Millicent besides the bank."

I'm awkwardly chuckling as the man shakes his head and leans in discreetly. "I shouldn't tell you this, but the guest goes by just the one name...*Ajax*. Is that familiar to you?"

What in the typhoid fever is happening? I clear my

throat, feeling like my mouth is suddenly dry. Did I just hallucinate? Did he just say...no, no way.

I'm plucking my shirt as I stare back, hearing him clicking more keys.

"Is it always this hot in February? Sorry, what did you say?"

He's staring at me, shitty news furrowing his brows as he remains quiet. "It seems as though Mr. Ajax had your name removed upon check-in. And a new lady friend added."

I can feel my grip tightening around the counter's edge as my brain calculates pi equals three point one forgive the fuck out of me. But what did he say?

He brought...to my vacation. He's here...in my room.

No. Fucking. Way.

My knees slowly begin to give in to an embarrassingly slow descent down into a squat as I hold tighter to the granite for dear life.

Who needs to stand when this is my rock bottom. I'm here. *Slay.*

From somewhere above comes, "Ma'am..." and "What is going on..." followed by, "Is she okay?"

I said Eat Pray Love, *but I got* Forgetting Sarah Marshall.

"Millie?"

Who said that?

Above me, words are being said, and conversations are being had, but me and my menty b are becoming better acquainted.

"Perhaps I could ring the room and we could straighten this out?"

"Straighten what out? What's wrong with the room?"

Maybe if I get close enough to the floor, it'll open up and welcome me inside the depths of this hell. Ajax is here. On our trip...on my trip.

"You don't have one. That's the issue. But I can offer you a single with a lovely view of our parking structure. I will warn the air-conditioning is currently out on that side of the hotel, but we are actively working on it."

Why. Why is this happening to me? I always take my shopping cart back and over-tip for my coffee. Where is my good karma?

"I thought you said you had a suite, Nate. We're gonna go ahead and go."

Great, even the rando brunettes are getting involved.

"We do. Stay. Come back."

"You don't."

No, he does. With his new girlfriend. We have a view of the parking structure. Maybe if I'm lucky, I can go stand at the entrance and get clipped by a car. Do they airlift off the island for crushed femurs?

Strong hands cup my armpits as I'm lifted back to my feet, and TJ's voice washes over me, breaking my descent into madness.

"On your feet, girlie. What's going on?"

"My ex stole my room."

As I'm answering, I hear my name.

It's in this very moment that I know in some past life, I've committed atrocities. The universe has been sitting and waiting for its moment to right the wrongs.

I turn around, my face void of the absolute gut punch I feel as I look directly into my ex's eyes.

"Mills? Is that you?"

Don't say my name like you know me, dick.

"Hey, Ajax."

My voice is uneven and too singsongy. I am not selling nonchalant. I'm selling hysteria.

TJ leans in over my head, speaking quietly to Nate as I take a half step forward.

"Ajax? That's his whole name? You gotta fucking be kidding me. That's what my meemaw tried sneaking into my awful-ass papaw's coffee to off him before someone explained divorce."

I hear Nate chuckle. "Well, now I guess we know Scrappy doesn't swallow."

There's plenty I have to say about that joke, but currently, I'm frozen in my damn place.

Arrested by the fact that my ex...whom I stood in front of...while practically nude...ready to blurt my innermost feelings...is standing in front of me.

With. Said. Girl.

At least this time, he isn't doing his best French impression.

"Wow," he says again, his eyebrows hitting his hair-line like he's so fucking shocked. "Sorry, *I'm* just so surprised to see you, babe...I mean, *we're* just so surprised to see you."

My eyes tick to where his hand is wrapped around her waist as he pulls her closer to his side. "Don't take this wrong, but what are you doing here?"

What am I doing here? What am. I. Doing here?

Other than participating in a social experiment judging how much humiliation one person can take before they turn to homicide?

I can't help myself and glance at his new girlfriend, who only seems interested in the giant trees behind me. She's stunning. I'd hoped it was my memory messing with me, but nope.

Against any and all social norms, I start to laugh to myself. Because I'm in fucking pajama pants. And a hoodie that smells like the cheesesteak I had on the plane. I mean, I guess it's a step up from whipped cream. But...is it?

For some reason, I thought I stepped forward, but now I can feel my arms touching Nate and TJ's. So maybe I'm walking backward since that's where my life seems to be headed.

"What do you mean why am I here?" I finally answer, bewildered. "I'm on vacation." I motion to TJ and Nate. "With *my* friends. Why are *you* on my vacation with *my* friends? And in *my* room...with...with..." I start snapping my fingers. "With your lady friend — "

Oh my god. I don't know Giselle Bundchen's name because I literally ran out that night.

Her shoulder pops brightly, oblivious to the tension growing in the air between me and my ex, pointing at herself. "Moonbeam."

A breathy "Right, sorry" is all I manage because I'm the asshole who can't think on her feet. Maybe the concierge will provide a new personality for the trouble caused by my displacement.

"No worries," she offers, playfully sticking out her tongue as she steps closer, twisting a lock of my hair around her finger. *What the hell?* "We didn't actually get to meet that night since you skedaddled so quickly. Shame because tu es magnifique. Maravilhosa. Gorgeous."

The amount of eye contact this girl's serving is unhinged.

I pull back, eyes searching the space because I'm in the sexual Twilight Zone.

Should I say thank you? What the hell does a person say at this moment? But before I can respond at all,

Moonbeam pushes herself across me, apparently done complimenting me in seventy-four languages, and extends a hand toward Nate.

"Oh, and we definitely didn't get to meet, handsome. I would've remembered you."

He looks down at her hand and then back at her face. "I'm good."

"Oh." She grins, retracting it, and winks. "Gotcha, big guy."

Gotcha? Got what. Got who. What is happening? None of this makes sense. Not one single fucking thing. How am I standing in some fucked-up parallel version of the most humiliating moment of my life?

My focus returns to Ajax, who's still standing there with that stupid fucking look on his face. There's so much I want to say, but the only thing that comes out is, "Answer my question. Why are you in my room, *Chad*?"

His eyes narrow at his real name. I didn't even realize I said it, but hooray ...*small victories*.

He releases Moonbeam, stepping forward to take my elbow, but before I even get the *No* out, TJ's nabbed his wrist.

"We're gonna keep our hands to ourselves, brother. Or playing with your little records is gonna get real tricky. Answer the question."

Chad pales. "I'd just like to speak to her privately if you don't mind." He looks at me as if I'm going to help him, cocking his head. "Babe?"

"Millie," Nate adds from the other side of me as he crosses his arms. "Don't talk to her like you know her."

Forget the twenty percent for being Uber drivers. I'll give them everything I own for this moment.

Chad takes his hand back, clearing his throat.

"Look, I texted a million times. And when you didn't respond, I assumed you weren't coming."

"Well, she's here now, dick," Nate levels.

I'm glaring at Chad but also berating myself for blocking his number. I can't believe I forgot to take his name off the room.

"Let's be real, Millie," he says way too snidely, ignoring Nate. "I figured it would be hard for you to be here with all the couples. Why would anyone come alone for Valentine's Day? Plus, you know I booked a gig here before we..." His voice trails off at the "broke up" part. "Hold on, is that why you're here? Did you come to try and get me back or something?"

I'm literally going to pop a blood vessel because what the fuck does he mean—GET. HIM. BACK.

I'd like to get him back in the ground like the fucking demon he is.

The smile on his face makes me want to punch him, especially when he looks at Moonbeam like they're sharing an inside joke.

You know in cartoons when someone eats something hot, and steam blows out of their ears and their head detaches and flies up? That's me. Internally.

"I apologize for the interjection," the hotel clerk says behind us, grabbing everyone's attention. "But would you three like the available room? Because it's the last one. Otherwise, we're completely sold out."

"Aww, fuck this," TJ mutters next to me.

My eyes grow even wider. Just when I think that's the worst part, the clerk adds, "And am I to still rebook the activities on the itinerary to Miss Moonbeam's name?"

Murderous. I'm truly fucking homicidal.

I paid for half of those. I did all the research to look up the fun shit. They're on my trip.

Everything stays on the tip of my tongue, unable to spill over as my fists ball at my sides and my chest heaves.

But inside my head sounds a bit like, *You stupid, shitty, flat-assed motherfucker. You kiss like your lips are scraping crumbs off a table. AND I FAKED ALL MY FUCKING ORGASMS.*

Silence grows as Chad and I wait for the other to speak first. But the only right answer is for him to give me my room back and go somewhere else...like maybe to hell. I hear it's warm.

As I open my mouth, his jaw tenses with a coldness. "My card's already on the reservation. And we checked in first. You'll have to take the other room. What do you need a suite for anyway? To binge *Gilmore Girls* again?" he chuckles. "It's just you, Millie. Don't be selfish."

I wish I were one of those girls who could think on their feet. Like Eleanor. I'm tempted to call her right now so she can stop having fancy Four Seasons sex with Crew and come downstairs to hand Chad his ass.

He deserves to have his handed to him.

"Baby—"

Baby?

My eyes lift to Nate, who is staring down at me. His fingers tuck my hair behind my ear. "Don't get worked up, Scrappy. Fuck him. We're good. He can have the room. We only need the bed anyway."

Uh? Hello? Am I breathing? I'm not even sure I have a pulse anymore. Wtf?

Fingers weave between mine on my other side just

before a soft kiss is pressed to the top of my hand, making me turn my head quickly, brows jumping up.

TJ grins down at me as he gives me a wink. "As long as you're between us. That's all I need for Valentine's Day."

What. The. Fuck.

I hear Chad say, "Hold on," but I can't stop volleying a smile between these two maniacal lifesavers.

Thank you, thank you, thank you, thank you.

I bite my lip before turning my focus back to Chad.

"So, no, *Chad.* I'm not here for you. But this was fun. Let's not do it again."

He moves Moonbeam off him as he looks between TJ and Nate before sounding way too accusatory and, frankly, ego-checked.

"You're with them...you're staying with *both* of them? Did this start in Vegas? Were you cheating on me?"

If I owned a cowboy hat, I'd throw it in the air right now. How does it feel, asshole? I turn back toward the counter, returning the small smile the clerk is giving as he slides my new keys to me.

TJ takes my hand, guiding it behind my back, pulling me flush to his front as he walks us backward and away from the scene of the crime.

Sarcasm rolls off his tongue in place of my silence as he whispers, "Ooo, Chad is mad," and laughs.

I look over my shoulder and see Nate standing in his place, slowly rubbing his hands together, just staring at my ex. As if at any minute, he might rush him and sack that piece of shit. And I'm positive it makes Chad nervous as hell. Although, I suppose a two-hundred sixty-five-pound defensive lineman would have that effect on everyone.

I grip TJ's hand harder because my feet feel clumsy around his as my face presses against his chest.

These two are so clutch right now, but I'm going to need a breather from real life. A drunken respite, for sure. I'm definitely skipping dinner tonight.

As if he already read my thoughts, the vibration of TJ's gravel pulses against my cheek as he speaks low, just for me to hear.

"He's still looking...still looking. Ten more feet, and you got a bottle of Jack with your name on it, Smalls. I got you. Trust me?"

All I can manage is a nod as I squeak out, "Tequila...I want tequila."

Even in what should feel like a victory, my stupid heart is beating too fast, and my throat feels tight because, for the next ten days, I get to watch what my future was supposed to look like while I rot in my present day.

Fuck. Chad. And fuck me.

four

. . .

"Girls do weird shit when they're sad."

tj

Nate stares at my profile as I grin from the lounge chairs that I procured. *Without* getting a thank-you from him.

"Did you text Crew or Eleanor?"

I shake my head. *Something tells me Millie wouldn't like that very much.* He lobs another question at me.

"But you let her go in...like that?"

I bite my bottom lip as I nod, staring at the feisty little one in question. "Yup."

He's still standing, looking at Millie in the pool, then back to me before he sits and points at her as if I don't know who he's talking about.

Oh, I know. She's hard to miss.

"Why would you let her go in like that? You asshole."

The smirk on my face isn't doing much to settle his ass down, but I still shrug out my honest answer.

28

"There wasn't any stopping her. It's not like she's gonna catch a cold."

The moment we hit the pool area and Millie was clear of Chad, she walked directly behind the bar and grabbed an entire bottle of Jose Cuervo before kicking off her shoes and traipsing directly into the pool...in all her clothes, even the damn hoodie.

I almost laugh again because the look on the bartenders' faces was priceless.

Nate claps his hands together, probably wishing they were around my neck.

"You're a professional fucking tight end, TJ. In the NFL. Your job is literally to block and catch. But you're telling me that girl got by you and walked into the goddamn pool. With all her clothes on. Holding...a bottle of booze. Without so much as a fingertip nabbing her?"

I stretch my arms, letting out a yawn before putting them behind my head.

"She also pushed some lady off that pink flamingo she's floatin' in. And if we're being technical, she stole the bottle. We just paid for it. Jail time felt like kicking her while she's down."

"Teej."

I laugh because he's barking now. I swear, one day, this dick is going to give himself a heart attack being such a control freak.

"Let her be, Nate. Her head is fucked-up, and girls do weird shit when they're sad. My sisters are proof. We're gonna wait her out because the sun is shining—" I raise a hand to the sky as, right on cue, the waiter approaches with two ridiculous drinks that look like sunrises. "—and look, we got drinks with little umbrellas in 'em."

I take mine and lift the toothpick, plucking off the

cherry between my teeth as I grin at my friend. His shoulders shake with a silent laugh as he finally relaxes on the chair, tossing the drink's fancy shit on the small table between us.

"All right. But when that tequila makes her think she's three feet taller than she is, you're going in after her, TJ. I'm not taking that scrappy little monster on. No fucking way."

"Gimme a break," I say confidently. "How bad could it be?"

"Not as bad as that fucking guy." Nate levels, looking at the drink before taking a swig. "I was about two seconds away from making him eat out of a straw."

"Same." I nod before looking at him with my brows raised. "We ever gonna tell Millie that Eleanor told us the whole story when it went down?"

"Nah," he breathes out as we both turn and watch her guzzle back tequila, almost falling off her floatie. "We'll save her dignity."

"You can't have it. It's mine."

Uh-oh. Yelling, accompanied by a shit ton of commotion, has me peeking one eye first before they both snap open. *Shit.* Two lifeguards are flanking Millie, clearly trying to coerce her out of the pool and off the flamingo, but by the looks of it, she's not going quietly.

I slap Nate in the chest. "Looks like Smalls is done being sad. She jumped right to rage."

"Yup," he draws out as we stand, stripping our T-shirts over our heads and making our way toward the throwdown.

And by throwdown, I mean Millie swinging her half-empty bottle of Cuervo as one of the attendants ducks, almost getting his bell rung.

"Damn. That woulda hurt." I chuckle, wading into the water as Nate smirks.

The water breaks against my thighs as we hear, "Ma'am, please," and "Jesus, be reasonable," followed by "Ow."

We stop about waist high in the pool, arms crossed, watching her reenact *King of the Mountain*, the pool version, as a slew of curses litter the sky. She dips into the water, almost falling off the flamingo, a long leg going one way as her head dips under the other. She flops back up, looking almost drowned with the soaked hoodie back on her head and half her bare leg showing in the pj pants.

"It's like trying to give a cat a bath," Nate muses.

I nod, wincing as her fist just misses the other guy. "And her claws are just as sharp."

"All right. That's enough of this shit," Nate grumbles, diving underwater as I make my way straight at her.

Mid-yell, her eyes lock to mine, and I'm pretty sure drunk Millie could rival some of the scariest linebackers out there.

"Ooo, girlie, this is gonna be fun," I whisper to myself just as Nate grabs the ass of the floatie and upends her, sending our feral kitty into the water.

"Scoop her up," he barks, turning toward the weary attendants. "We'll leave something at the front to make up for your trouble."

They nod as I haul Millie out of the water, hands

under her armpits, body dangling like a hanging piece of laundry, so we're face-to-face.

"Time to go, Ariel. How are the legs? You walking or crawling outta here?" Water's dripping like rain around her face as she hiccups. "That's what I thought."

Up and over my shoulder she goes, and I carry a very drunk Millie out of the pool. But the minute I hit dry ground, she smacks my ass and yells.

"Nate, don't forget my pink chicken."

Another hiccup, followed by Nate's growl as he goes back for the flamingo floatie, has me laughing. We might be in over our heads with this one.

But damn, she keeps it interesting. There's something about girls with buns as messy as their lives. That's for sure.

five

· · ·

"I don't mean the three minutes in heaven
he's been delivering."

millie

Pounding...thunderous pounding has taken up residence inside my head like a million tiny jack-hammers punching holes in my frontal lobe, and it seems to be getting worse with every inch I open my eyes.

"Ouch," I whisper, immediately choking from the driest mouth in history before I reach for the water bottle next to my bed.

I barely get the cap off before guzzling it down to empty. Kind of like I did with the bottle of tequila yesterday.

"Oh god," I breathe out, my hands coming to my head. "Why did I do that? Stupid. So dumb."

It takes a few very slow scoots of my body, but I manage to sit up, letting out a measured whoosh of air as I adjust the sheet around me. It's nice. *There must be a really high thread count.* Hold up a minute.

33

I still, eyes shifting side to side, taking in my surroundings.

I'm in a bed. In a room...*a hotel room.*

My stomach roils as I timeline yesterday and last night. It takes me a minute, but it's all there. Agonizingly there.

Chad. Moonbeam.

The pool.

My meltdown over a flamingo floatie.

TJ carrying me back to the room. And Nate finally caving and calling Eleanor to help me change into dry pajamas because I refused to let anyone *touch* me as I lay on the bathroom floor *making drunk water angels.*

Jesus Christ.

My eyes squeeze closed, viscerally feeling the regret. I really need to stop embarrassing myself in front of every single person I know.

A heavy breath leaves me as I shift my legs off the bed, feet on the Berber before I stand, slowly. God, maybe this hangover will do me in before I have to face anyone.

I swipe my phone off the nightstand before I take a few aided steps, each feeling slow because death really knows how to cripple your vibe.

As if to add insult to injury, as soon as I open the bedroom door, I'm hit with the scent of bacon, making my stomach turn again.

"Oh gross," I groan, holding back what's left in my belly, placing a palm on it.

"Mornin', sunshine," TJ greets, looking up from where he's lying on a cot with his head on the infamous pool floatie.

In what might be the smallest hotel living room I've ever seen.

34

Not that I'm focused on that because he's shirtless in jade swim trunks. His feet are planted on each side of the makeshift bed, with a piece of bacon suspended above his bare chest, awaiting his chomp.

"Didn't have a pillow?" I point to the flamingo.

"Freddie," he tosses out quickly.

"What?"

TJ motions behind him, using a new piece of bacon. "We named him Freddie."

I chuckle, wincing before I look away because watching him chew is making me queasy.

Nate extends a cup of coffee from the chair (nope, that's the couch) he's lounging in as he smirks. He's also shirtless, with a towel wrapped around his waist, one of his intricately tatted thighs peeking out. They're beckoning me to be crushed by them.

Good god, I don't have the energy for this.

Nate being sexy while I actively die is fucking rude.

"It's got a little kick," he offers. I instantly smell the Baileys. "Hair of the dog. Don't complain. Just drink it."

I don't complain. I happily take it and sip as I make my way to the couch-chair in the too-bright living room and perch on the arm.

"Blinds. Please," I mutter, but TJ is already carrying his plate of pig over to the window to close them.

Nate chuckles. "I'd ask how you're feeling, but it's pretty obvious."

Another appreciative sip and I look up at him.

"Yeah, but what you don't see is the deep, sorrowful embarrassment I feel. You guys, I'm so sorry you had to handle me yesterday. But...thank you."

TJ scoffs as he sits back down on his jail bed.

"Smalls, you ain't got nothing to apologize for. Sometimes your heart needs more time to accept what your mind already knows."

Whoa. Nate and I both stare at TJ, surprised by his sudden depth and poetry.

"Where'd you hear that? Did you read that in a book?" Nate tosses out, but without missing a beat, TJ answers, "Pinterest."

I laugh, then grimace because, fuck, my head.

"So, this is our room?" I commiserate only because they have eyes.

They nod, staring at me with the same *this sucks* look on their faces.

I grimace. "I should be swimming in my infinity pool. Listening to the waves crash against whatever they crash into."

TJ hums an agreement as Nate pipes up. "At least you had a bed. I'm six foot six. I was cradled by wood all night. You know how fucking hard it is to sleep when you have no feeling in your feet cuz they're hanging off the side of the chair?"

"It's a couch," TJ throws out, but I cut him off.

"There has to be another room. Or another hotel."

A memory of Vegas with me and Eleanor pops into my mind, making me half laugh. What is with my luck with hotels?

I lean forward to grab the phone I put down on the table so I can text her what I was just thinking when I notice a message from an unknown number.

TJ starts complaining about the heat, saying something about naked ice cube parties, but I'm not listening because my adrenaline has begun to course through my veins like the 'roids they give racehorses to make them win the Derby.

I might even be foaming at the mouth too.

> 662-465-1234: Hey, just in case you have me blocked I'm texting from Moon's phone. Millie, you mean so much to me and I know today was hard. But you don't have to do this. Turning yourself into some kind of cleat chaser isn't the look. I will always feel something for you, but I can't be with someone who doesn't respect themselves. Manifesting clean vibes and light. xx—A

"Did I just get broken up with by the villain on *Pretty Little Liars*?"

The thought begins as a barely audible whisper, only to grow louder and louder until the last part is a scream.

"Did I...just get broken up with...by PRETTY LITTLE LIARSSSS?"

TJ fumbles the plate on his chest, jump scared, bacon flying everywhere as Nate bounds up, looking around with his fists up like he's going to fight whoever's breaking in.

"What the fuck?" ... "What's happening?"

The effort in which I try and twist my phone into metal bits makes my muscles immediately sore, and all the curses spewing out sound guttural and mangled.

"Stupid-fuck-shit-asshole-dumbshit-mother-I-already-broke-up-with-you-fucker..."

Whatever hangover I was suffering from is gone because I've been healed by rage.

"Millie. What the fuck, you good?" Nate tosses out, but I don't stop trying to kill my phone.

TJ picks up his plate, staring at me. "Smalls. What the fuck is going on?"

I hurl my phone down onto the couch seat and stand, breathless, hair in disarray as I stare between them. My face is hot, and my entire body feels explosive. Actually… my stomach rolls. And I feel it.

Fuck.

I cup my mouth as I try and utter words. But it's no use. I'm about to add tequila to the list of things I'll never do again. I take off toward the bathroom, busting through my room until I'm worshipping the porcelain on my knees.

Everything I've ever eaten since I was ten, even if it's only a memory, tries to eject itself from my body. My hair is pulled back away from my face as my body commits to cat back.

I breathe, settling back, half shrieking to whoever's holding my hair, "Don't look at me."

I puke again.

"Jesus, Nate…call a priest. I think I saw pea soup."

Oh god. It's TJ, not him. Please, god, he'll never not make jokes about this.

I'm breathing harder as I finish. "Go away. Let me die in peace."

He sweeps a fallen strand back over my cheek to join the others in his hand.

"You want just me to leave? Or should I take the father, son, and holy spirit with me?"

I am in hell.

"TJ," I grit out, but it comes out in a burp, followed by vomit, making me sound like a real demon.

The way the two of them start laughing cements that I'm going to change my name and move to an undisclosed location where cell phones and visitors are discouraged. Like a prison.

With my eyes closed, I hold in place, waiting, making sure I'm really deficient in all nutritional substances before I finally sit back on my haunches and close the lid.

I'm handed a tissue, so I wipe my mouth and add it before flushing.

Please let this be rock bottom and not a trapdoor that just leads to another.

TJ lets go of my hair and helps me stand before I make my way out of the toilet. His hand rubs gentle circles on my back as we walk to the sink. It doesn't even leave as I rinse my mouth.

And as much as ten seconds ago I wanted to escape ever being in the same room with him again, this is comforting.

"Thank you for holding my hair."

He smirks down at me, following me into the bedroom, where Nate's pulled the blanket back and put a new bottle of water by my bed.

"Is there a contest going on for best hotel roomies? Because you guys win," I offer quietly, climbing in and sighing as Nate puts a cool washcloth on my head.

"We're just scared you might levitate."

I smile and try not to laugh as I take a few steady breaths. They take up posts at the bottom of the bed as I look between them. For the first time, I say exactly what I'm thinking when I'm thinking it.

"I fucking hate him...Chad. He just keeps ruining my life. First, he cheats. And not just cheats...that asshole walked in—"

Nate rubs the top of my foot under the blanket. "We already know."

"Dude," TJ presses, giving him a look like they'd talked about that.

But Nate shrugs, answering the look. "This is saving her dignity."

I don't even care that they know. I'm happy to not have to repeat it ever again. My shoulders pop a shrug as I lick my dry lips.

"Well then, you get how fucked this whole situation is. And the rub is that, now, he's here, all up in my face. Living his best life...the one I planned for him. On our trip with his glow-up multilingual cunnilinguist. And I'm a drunken mess who started a WWE match in the pool with a floatie."

They're nodding, looking equally as irritated, but I don't stop.

"I just wish I could ruin his trip. Make him just as miserable as me. Shit all over his Valentine's the way he ruined my New Year's."

"Yeah," Nate commiserates. "We should be popping bottles and babes. Not dying of heat exhaustion in this room while he lives the life."

We're sitting in silence, stewing until TJ gives a toothy grin.

"We should fuck Chad."

My eyes pop back open as Nate's head whips to TJ's, and we both speak at the same time. "Hard pass, Teej." ... "It's a no for me, but go off."

TJ laughs, waving us off. "No, guys—" He looks at me. "I don't mean the three minutes in heaven he's been delivering. I mean we should actually ruin his trip. Screw that guy. It's only fair since he ruined ours."

I look around the room, already feeling sweaty from the lack of air-conditioning and not because I'm going to puke.

Chad deserves this. Revenge with a capital fucking *R*.

The washcloth on my head hits the floor before I sit up, smiling as I look between them.

"So, what's the plan?"

six

. . .

"I've entered my villain era. Hi, happy to be here."

millie

"A throuple?" TJ smirks as I repeat it again. "A fake *throuple*. Out in public. Are you serious?"

I dramatically blink once and pause because that is not what I thought he was going to say. A bag of crabs mysteriously finding their way into Chad's room. All his reservations canceled. That's what I was thinking. But this? What?

"As a heart attack," he says with so much confidence I feel stupid for even asking. "I told you I got sisters. I've been in the war room. Girls love revenge, and mine brought me up right." I laugh because he's so silly it's hard not to as he continues. "There ain't nothing a dude hates more than someone else fucking with his shit. He's already proven himself to be no exception. Now, times that by two. It's competition 101."

"I'm *shit* in this metaphor?" I'm shaking my head, but

TJ smiles, throwing back a play on his words. "You are *the shit.*"

"*Ohhkay,*" I say back mockingly, hiding my grin.

Nate points at him before half lying on the bed, his feet on the ground.

"TJ's right. You just didn't notice because you were in your head yesterday. But that asshole was so pissed when he thought you were staying with us. He's already bought it."

I chew the inside of my cheek, fanning myself. God, we need air-conditioning. The idea is rumbling around, making a petty smile take root on my lips before I suddenly remember what that fucking text said.

Oh damn. They're right. It wasn't a fleeting reaction. Chad is bothered.

"You're right," I breathe out. "He called me a cleat chaser—"

"What the fuck," they both bellow, but I just nod.

"Grab my phone. Look at the text from the unknown number. He is mad… Chad. Is. Mad."

TJ's up and jogging to grab it before he walks back, reading it aloud. Nate's eyes stay locked on mine the whole time until TJ finishes, and then he growls.

"When I see that motherfucker, it's on sight, Mills."

I let out a cracked whip of a laugh. "No, for real. What a dick, right?"

Nate nods before he smacks the bed and stands. "Yeah. I hate that guy. No side of the pillow should ever be cold."

"Every STD should be caught."

Nate laughs, deep and baritone, but TJ looks less amused.

TJ's hand is gripped on the back of his neck as he

places my phone beside me. "Fuck that. 'Clean vibes and light'... Naw, men don't speak to women this way. I'm gonna go get his room number. We're about to see him now. Nate, come on."

TJ spins toward the door, Nate joining, but I scramble to my knees and call out, half laughing, half swooning.

Is this my live version of "we're gonna hurt some people...whose car are we taking" Ben Affleck moment? *Praise be.*

"Wait. No—" TJ's hand is gripping the doorframe as they look over their massive shoulders, and I smile. "If you go to jail, then I'm a prison princess...or whatever they call girls who date felons. I need my fake boyfriends on the outside. Because I think this could work."

I shuffle on my knees to the end of the bed, hand on my tummy to keep it settled, my eyes on theirs.

"You said we'd be everywhere they are. Like white on rice. A constant reminder that I leveled up, right?"

TJ nods, walking back over, followed by Nate, until they're standing in front of me.

"I'll see that and raise you one. If it's not me he's jealous over"—I point between them—"then you two can charm the bikini bottoms off Moonbeam."

Matching smiles bloom on their faces as I continue. "Shit, maybe she'll kick him out of the room, and we can all get our beds back."

TJ grins at me, teasing. "Nate can handle Moonpie. She was pretty into him anyway."

Beam, I mouth, feeling like I've entered my villain era. *Hi, happy to be here.*

Nate scoffs like he pulled the short stick before I chuckle. I always say that the universe gives you what you need. And apparently, what I *need* is a fake three-way to mend my broken heart. *Two dicks in order to get over one.*

I ease myself to sitting before I stand, extending a hand for each of them to shake.

"Are we all in? Are we really doing this?"

TJ double slaps my hand like we're on the field, making me laugh as he says, "We're gonna have some fun."

Nate shakes the other gently. "We're getting our damn vacation back."

Never did I ever think this is what my week would look like, but I already wholeheartedly prefer this to the alternative.

"Perfect. Then, first up is a club. Downtown. His friend is spinning."

TJ swipes my phone back up off the bed. "We're booking a table. I'm getting all the damn bottles." His eyes dart up to mine with his signature smirk. "By the way, what kind of Bambi doesn't put a lock on her phone?"

I hold up my hands. "I have nothing to hide. Other than my fake relationship and the nudes I took last week."

TJ raises his brows as I mouth, *Kidding*, just as Nate's fingers come under my chin, lifting my face to his.

"Scrappy, if we're clubbing, you're gonna need to look hot. Like hotter than hot."

"Hotter than hot. I can do that."

TJ grins up from my phone, holding up a picture of me in a bikini.

"We believe in you, Smalls. Now, show us what you got."

seven

. . .

"If your liver ain't showing, it's not short enough."

nate

"Millie. Come on," I shout, looking over at TJ, who's sitting in Freddie as I grumble. "She's been in there forever."

He just laughs before he clears his throat, looking up from his phone.

"Crew and Elle want us to meet them at two o'clock for lunch since they just got up. Said to bring Mills."

I smile, realizing what he just said. "Damn, it's eleven thirty, and they just got up? Those two are gonna fuck each other to death before they make it down the aisle...*again*."

TJ cracks his neck. "Worse ways to die."

We're both laughing as the bedroom door finally swings open, and Millie steps out, arms splayed, popping her hips side to side.

"Whaddya think? Scorching, right? He's gonna need a cold shower."

Oh shit.

TJ's face swings to mine as we give each other a look like *"fuck"* before we turn back to Millie. This is one of those questions that dudes can't answer honestly because no matter how we frame the truth, she's not going to like it.

"What?" she rushes out, running her hands down her waist, reading the room too well.

My eyes fix on her body for a little too long. But, shit, I'm human, and she's hot. Always has been.

How that idiot didn't ask for seconds when she dessert barred him is beyond me. What guy turns her down? No guy...just Ajax. *Stupid fucking name.*

"How is this not hot?" she levels, hands on her hips now.

When I said hot, I meant *all* the assets on display, not zero of them. And frankly, she's got assets. But I swear girls have a different dictionary. It's like whatever we say has a completely different meaning in their heads.

That's the only explanation for this outfit.

Millie's standing here in one of those tight black skirts that go to the knee and have a slit halfway up the thigh. Don't get me wrong, she's a ten. Especially in that cropped T-shirt that shows off her stomach. But...

Millie crosses her arms, a sure sign of warfare.

"My whole leg is showing...and most of my body. How is this not hot?"

TJ licks his lips, saying nothing, just grinning like the asshole he is.

He's going to leave me out in the wind. *Dick.* My brows furrow, but instinctively, I hold up a hand because that's what you do when an attack is imminent.

"Mills, this is said in the spirit of teamwork." I run a

hand down my jaw, trying to make all the humor I'm feeling over the way she's glaring at me disappear. "We're all on the same side here. Right?" Her brows raise as he huffs. *Shit.* "Here's the thing, Millie. See, as a man—"

I don't get the rest out before TJ cuts in. "You gotta look skanky, baby. If your liver ain't showing, it's not short enough."

Jesus. Christ.

My face whips to his, the shock apparent. I always knew he'd be the reason we die.

Here lies TJ and Nate, death by the former's country ass's audacity.

There's a beat of silence before he shrugs and puts his hands behind his head. I laugh to myself, looking down at my lap for a moment. I swear only he could get away with this shit.

"Come on." She exhales. "I totally look *down to…*" She leaves off the *fuck*, making both of us clear our throats.

I turn my attention back to Millie and jump back in, building off what my asshole best friend just said.

"See, cuz, Mills. Right now, you're not though. You're beautiful. Classy. Sexy."

She narrows her eyes. How is she offended by that? I swear, you ask any woman, "Would you rather be right or happy," and she'll answer, "I'm happy when he knows I'm right."

TJ falls in, tag teaming the moment. "This outfit says dream girl material, Millie."

Her lips purse.

I nod, biting my bottom lip. "Exactly."

Damn, she's a hard nut to crack, but that won't stop us. We have a mission to complete, and fashion isn't going to stop us.

I look at TJ, motioning to him like *the floor is yours, buddy*.

Because if there's one thing I can count on, it's TJ doing what he does best—charming that skirt right off that girl.

"Here's the thing, darlin'. You look like the kind of girl who has good credit."

Oh shit. He pulled out the darlin'. My turn.

I chuckle. "Yeah. Like a woman who reads and has a library card."

She sucks her bottom lip between her teeth.

Is that a smile you're hiding? Come on, Scrappy. Let it out.

TJ grins, continuing with our bullshit. "You look like someone who gives blood every year."

I nod, rubbing my chest. "Like a girl who lets someone cut her in line at the grocery store when they only have one item."

She presses her lips together, this time trying not to laugh. So I can't help myself, adding extra.

"Scrappy, you look like the kind of girl my mom would *want* me to meet."

Millie finally busts into a small laugh before shaking her head at us, saying exactly what we're thinking.

"Okay. I get it. I'm hot. But what we need is hooker. Respectfully."

"Respectfully," TJ and I add together.

She frowns and looks down at her outfit before looking back at us and winks.

"Then I guess we're going shopping. Let's hoe me up."

eight

. . .

"It's like a horny contact high."

millie

Two hours and three hundred and fifty-seven thousand outfits later, I have a dress. And not just any dress. I'm pretty sure I lost feeling in my torso from how tight the corset was.

However, judging by how the guys adjusted in their seats and couldn't make eye contact with me, I think it's a winner.

God, the petty betty in me cannot wait for Chad to see me tonight. For him to be reminded of exactly what he lost. And what he'll never get back.

My eyes tick up to the boys.

"Hey, thanks again for walking me to the room to put my dress up. I guess chivalry's not dead. Although," I joke, "you did pick out my outfit, so maybe it is. I'm still unconvinced the skirt isn't a tube top."

TJ winks, but Nate looks amused. "Maybe don't bend over?"

50

Oh my god.

I smirk, looking down for a second, wondering if my toenails will match as I speak. "That's probably a good idea because I don't think I can wear any underwear." The elevator dings for the bottom floor. "Or maybe a thong? I could cosplay *Euphoria*."

My head lifts, shifting to TJ's as the doors slide open.

He's frozen with half a smirk on his face, his mouth opening, then closing like he can't get any words out.

"Girl," he draws out, his hand holding the door open.

I smile, taking a step forward, only to blanch because I'm suddenly staring directly into a set of familiar blue eyes.

Yuck.

"Hey, lovers," comes from Chad's side. But I don't say anything back to him and Moonbeam as they make room for us to exit.

"Sunshine…dickhead," TJ greets as Nate pulls me behind him.

"Moonbeam," she purrs as we walk past.

I don't know when Nate took my hand, but I'm grateful because I secretly wish I was bold enough to pop Chad right in the jaw. I mean, if he's going to take my room and all my plans, he might as well catch these hands too.

"Millie. I texted you…" Chad calls, but a tug on my hand snaps my focus to Nate's voice.

"Ignore him. And work those hips."

TJ's arm drapes over my shoulders as he looks down at me with a grin. "Oh, he's hating life right now."

Fuck being a cleat chaser—suit me all the way up, Coach. Because I'm about to score a fucking touchdown. *Is that a football thing?*

I turn my head toward Nate to say something celebratory just as TJ squeezes my side. But apparently, Nate had a different idea because I'm immediately face-to-face with his lips.

Ohmygod.

I squeal and jerk back, surprised, as I immediately hear, "Fuck," behind me. Because I've just hit the back of my head on whatever part of TJ's face that was also attempting to love-bomb me.

"Sorry. Sorry." My eyes pop open, and I cover the back of my head with my palm as I spin between them. "You guys. I'm so sorry."

I look up to apologize again, half laughing, but panic sets in because their heads are whipped back over their shoulders toward the elevator doors.

Which are now closed.

I almost breathe a sigh of relief until I notice it's only moving to the second floor.

"Shit," I whisper. "You don't think they saw, do you?"

"Saw what? Me almost losing a tooth?" TJ humors back, swiping a finger over his bottom lip and checking for blood. "No, we're good."

I wince, feeling guilty, especially since I can't help the way my shoulders shake as I reach up, lifting his lip to ensure all TJ's teeth are, in fact, present and accounted for.

Nate chuckles, running a hand through his dark black hair. "Why'd you freak out, weirdo? I was just kissing the side of your head."

I swing back around to Nate, feeling slightly embarrassed and overly aware that I'm blushing as I toss my hands in the air.

"You snuck up on me. Like a ninja attack. I didn't even

know that was on the table. I thought we were *pretending* to date."

He cocks his head, grinning as if to say a loaded, "*Yeah*."

My eyes narrow, not because I'm mad, but because I just heard what I said out loud. I'm an idiot.

"I told you I crumble under pressure. I said I was a bad liar."

Nate rubs his jaw as he starts to laugh.

"No...you left that part out when we concocted a whole plan reliant on lying and thriving under pressure."

My mouth drops open, feigning shock, as if this is all news to me. Until TJ tickles my side, making me jerk my body into an awkward, bendy contraction accompanied by a half-grunted laugh.

"Quit it," I chuckle, slapping his hands. "Fine. I thought I would be better at this because I was fueled by villainous rage. Clearly, I was wrong." Their eyebrows rise. "But we're here. So..."

I hate that they're so amused, both staring at me, arms crossed, making me even more nervous about what I'm about to say.

"So...*what*?" TJ smirks.

I take a deep breath. "Sooo...kiss me. Let's just rip the Band-Aid off."

I lift my hands, giving a *come here* motion like in a Bruce Lee movie before he takes on six dudes.

Except I'm only tongue wrestling two, so why does this seem impossible?

TJ looks at Nate, who just shrugs. So, he nods, looking around the lobby before stepping forward, closing in on me. *Ooo. Why is my heart beating so fast?*

It's just a kiss.

I mean, yes, TJ's hot, but this means nothing. It's like when actors do it. TJ just has to be my Zack Galifianakis. Cool guy, but I wouldn't date him.

Except when he leans down and the smell of his minty breath gets close enough to tickle my skin, I fold my palm over his face before I spin away, making space between us.

"Okay..." I laugh, feeling the flush up my whole neck. "Maybe we start somewhere else?"

"Mills," TJ laughs, being unfunny funny. "You have kissed somebody before? Right? Like Chad's crossed that line?"

"Oh my god," I draw out dramatically, looking around to make sure nobody heard him. Suddenly, I catch Eleanor and Crew walking toward the restaurant where we're supposed to be meeting them.

Fuck.

I reach for TJ's hand, only nabbing his finger—his middle one, which is longer and bigger than I anticipated.

The tingles that hit my body are embarrassingly sponsored by dirty thoughts: creating thirsty women everywhere.

I spin around gently, tugging that damn finger quickly, forcing me—*all of us*—over behind a bank of tall plants.

"Huddle up," I whisper-bark, speaking their language.

Nate chuckles as they close in, surrounding me with their bodies and their man scents. God, they really do smell so fucking good. I love the way men's cologne just infiltrates your nose and travels all the way down to your uterus.

It's like a horny contact high.

This is the sole reason women have an "almost baby daddy, but we're not together" story.

"What are we doing?" TJ whispers, his hazel eyes sparkling.

But Nate roasts me. "Not making out."

"Shush," I level, shoving their unmovable shoulders. "I think…I think we should hang out."

They look at each other, then back to me, before Nate points at the plants. "Behind these trees?"

TJ looks over his shoulder, then grins. "Are we posting up for the whole day or just for now?"

I'll kill them.

"Will you be serious for one minute?" I know I'm smiling, and that's not helping me whip them into shape. "What I mean is that we should cancel lunch with the lovebirds and spend the day together. Get to know each other better. Because then I think I'd be less nervous or intimidated by this—" I motion between them. "This whole extra dude thing."

TJ frowns, crossing his arms. "Which one of us is the extra, exactly?"

I almost laugh because guys always focus on the wrong parts of a conversation. Ignoring him, I shove my hands in the back pockets of my shorts.

"If we get to know each other, it won't feel so much like a first date." My eyes meet Nate's. "And then you can be flirty and touchy-feely without us having to worry about TJ losing his teeth."

TJ's brows rise, and I can see the joke.

"Above-the-waist touching," I warn, but his smile doesn't go away. "And below the chest." He laughs as my voice grows more rushed. "All the non-fun parts." I sigh before joining in the laughter. "If we're going to sell this, it has to stop being awkward. *I* have to stop being awkward. And you two could make a fucking nun nervous."

I bite my bottom lip because they're just staring at me again in that way I'm starting to recognize as Tweedle bullshit time.

I'm about to be verbally tag teamed.

Nate grins. "So, what you're saying is you think we're superhot?"

I immediately turn around like I'm going to leave, but TJ loops a finger through the belt loop on my shorts, dragging me back as he says, "So hot you can't take your eyes off us?"

Nate cocks his head and bends sideways so that I'm forced to look at him.

"How long have you felt this way, Mills?"

TJ jerks my pants, making me shake as I laugh.

"Yeah, because I feel really objectified."

I'm finally released, so I spin around, putting my hands on my hips, but Nate locks eyes with me.

"I'm more than my muscles." *Don't discount those thighs, Nate.*

Gah, they're too much. As is the smile on my face, and it's not leaving anytime soon. But I press forward anyway.

"Are you going to tell me what you think about what I proposed or not?"

TJ throws his arm around me. "Well, I need my teeth, so I vote yes to flirting with my girl all day."

I quietly laugh, loving that he jumped right in before we both look at Nate.

"Okay. We'll follow your lead, baby."

There's that baby again.

I let out a whoosh of breath and reach into my back pocket, pulling out my phone as I text Eleanor while speaking to the boys.

"Also, we don't tell Eleanor or Crew. We're keeping it to ourselves." I lift my eyes to theirs. "Otherwise, they'll never let us live this down. Plus, if we can sell it to them, our best friends, then we can sell it to anyone."

Mills: Hey, happy early V-day present from me to you. Let's meet tonight for the club. Have fun getting pregnant before the wedding.

Elle: Noooooo. But okaaaayyyyy. What are you going to do though? I'm not leaving you stranded. Chicks before dicks.

Mills: The boys got me. Remember.

Elle: HOLD THE LINE. EXPLAIN NOW

Mills: *kisses

Elle: Are you having your very own little homance?

Mills: What?

Elle: A holiday romance.

Elle: Duh. You're not going to answer this, are you?

Elle: Bitch.

Elle: Come back...cum on your back. Haha byeeeee.

nine

. . .

"I wanna fuck your sister."

tj

"What are we doing again?"

Millie's had me and Nate lying on the beach for the last ten minutes doing some wild shit with the crystals she bought after our sneak-away lunch.

She bats her lashes at me before removing my sunglasses and feathering my lids closed. I take a deep breath, feeling a cold rock placed on my forehead.

"This is an amethyst." Her voice is quiet, and I know she's grinning. Because she's been doing that all afternoon. "It helps open your third eye and make us spiritually connected. Which is perfect for tonight."

I hum my understanding, but Nate grumbles next to me.

"Just what I've always wanted. To work on my spiritual connection with TJ."

"Really?" Her voice is so hopeful, and it's fucking killing me because he immediately growls.

"No, woman. What the hell do you have us doing out here? We're outside."

I don't have to open my eyes to know Nate absolutely does not have his closed. And he is definitely not lying on his beach towel with a fucking purple crystal on his forehead. He's such a grumpy asshole.

I can't hold it in, and I laugh too loud. Too hard. My stomach contracts, lifting me up.

"Don't move," she squeals, putting her hand on my chest, but I nab it, bringing it to my mouth and nipping the side.

"Stop," she laughs, tugging it away before going in on Nate. "Would you stop being such a baby? This is important. The sun is almost setting. You need to take the sun into your body through the crystal. I already explained this."

"I'm not taking anything inside my damn body. Millie—"

I feel her squirm as she giggles, Nate growling in the background.

The whole afternoon's been just like this. Us flirting with her, being handsy while she giggles and blushes. Basically, being horndogs while Millie's fucking adorable.

I'll give it to her. It was a good idea to get to know each other because I already knew she was cool and funny. And obviously hot. Now I know she's quirky, with the kind of unguarded smile that makes you want to remember what her favorite flower is.

But what I didn't expect was how much chemistry we'd have. And by we, I mean the three of us. It's weird to think, but it's like I can't get near her without that immediately calling to Nate and vice versa.

The feeling is raw, a kind base pull of our instincts. And it hasn't mattered if she's on my lap or walking with his hand slung over her shoulders. Millie's been content in the middle of our orbit.

And *that's* fucking with my head.

"How do you put up with him?" she fake complains.

My stone's removed before she places my sunglasses back on, smacking Nate's hand away again. I prop myself up on my elbow smirking.

"It's a real challenge. But I'm happy my heroism is finally being acknowledged."

A breeze lifts a strand of her hair off her shoulder as she licks her lips. Goddamn, she's effortlessly sexual. How the fuck did that dude fumble the ball so hard? What a dick.

"All right, we did your crystal thing." I pat her thigh, wishing I could slide my hand higher. "Now you have to answer some of our burning questions."

She swipes up her smoothie, toying with the straw between her teeth, making a little crunch sound. "Go ahead. Shoot."

My eyes are instantly on her lips.

The shit I would do to your mouth.

I'm lost in dirty thoughts, worried I'll need to go hide in the water for a few minutes when her tongue joins, circling the rim as her eyes meet mine.

Fuck me.

That's the closest I've been to popping off in my pants since puberty.

Nate reaches out just as fast as I do to take her drink away, but she dodges us.

"Not sharing," she rasps. "Ask your questions, and stop trying to steal my peach sensation."

Come the hell on. Peach sensation? *Lemme fuck that peach.*

I clear my throat, trying not to laugh at my own joke because I'd never cross a line with her. Unless she wanted to. Which is unlikely, considering I'm pretty sure she's still in a "hate all men" phase. Which is…fair.

Doesn't mean I'm not going to make her squirm though.

"What do you have against sharing?" I say, letting my voice stay nice and gravelly, hoping I make the right parts of her pay attention.

I'm staring into her eyes, letting the innuendo sit, with a smirk at her opened-mouth smile.

I know she knows about us.

Her eyes divert toward the water as she takes another sip. But then she grins, facing us again. I can see her gathering her nerve before she answers.

And it's fucking cute.

"Nothing, actually. To be fair, I've never partaken." Her eyes shift between us before she stands at the very edge of flirtation, then jumps. "But I hear you two excel at it."

Oh damn, I love it when she flirts back like this. Girl's got game.

"Perfect," Nate growls, snatching her drink. "Then you don't mind if we finish your peach off together."

She squeals and covers her face, beaten into dirty submission. He chuckles, then takes a swig and passes it over to me. I can't help but smile as we watch her scrunch her nose, embarrassed.

Damn, she's easy to like.

I hand the smoothie back to her, licking the leftover off my lip. It garners a wink as she sticks her tongue out sideways before glancing down at her straw. The thought is all over her face until finally, she lowers her sunglasses and gives in, gently placing her lips where ours were and sips.

Look at you being brave. Smalls, I'd break you in so slow. Fuckkk.

She turns around and lies on her towel, baking between us, but there's a crackle in the air, and I know she feels it too. It's hard to miss.

For a beat, the only sounds are the ocean, sporadic laughter from around us, and the occasional seagull. That is until she breaks the silence.

"So, is *that* the only way you guys...you know? Or do you have separate interests too?"

The question feels like a live wire.

A smile creeps out onto my face. But I say nothing, letting Nate answer. His voice is steady, like it's the most natural thing for her to ask.

"It's not the singular way. We have separate interests. We just like it best."

I sit up, grabbing her smoothie and seeing her make a little "oh" with her mouth. She's scraping her bottom lip with her teeth, chewing on the next question.

"Then how come you don't date the girls you share? Since you like doing it so much."

I lie down on my side, eyes lingering over her before I'm suddenly fixated on a patch of sand stuck to her stomach.

"It's too complicated," I whisper, bringing a finger to it and drawing a tiny infinity circle. "Pussy's one thing. Someone's heart is different."

Goose bumps pebble her skin. So I lift my finger, but neither Nate nor I miss the way she quietly gasps at the loss. *Oh damn.*

In a flash, she shoves her sunglasses onto her head, sitting up, not looking at us.

"I think I'm gonna go in the water."

Neither one of us answers as we watch her shimmy off her jean shorts and stand.

For fuck's sake.

My eyes are glued to her, and so are Nate's as she walks toward the water.

Because Millie is in a hot pink, ass-out bikini bottom. Whoever is in charge upstairs hates me. Nate growls, throwing sand at me.

"Your plan is a fucking death sentence."

I laugh because I get it as I dust off my lap. "Yeah, I don't live, laugh, love this for us either, brother."

"Teej, I feel like a predator. All I can think about is her peach sensation. We're supposed to be getting revenge. Not laid."

I scratch my stubbly beard, almost just talking to myself. "She's just one of the guys. A little sister. We're just gonna keep telling ourselves that."

But as I say it, Millie runs her fingers under the strings on her hips before looking at us over her shoulder.

Nate groans. "I wanna fuck your sister."

I fall back onto the towel. "Fuck you. Why would you say that? I just thought *me too.* And now I'm gonna need therapy."

Nate stands, making me start to do the same as he laughs. "We should think about our grandmas. That'll help. Right? Keep us on track."

I lock eyes with him. "Mine's dead."

"Even better."

We both grin, knowing there's no cure for what we got, before taking off, ninety miles an hour right for her.

"No. No. Noooo," she squeals before I scoop her up and throw us both right into the water.

And all I can think is she may have never partaken... The rest leaves my lips in my best *Dazed and Confused* impression. "But it'd be a lot cooler if she did."

ten

. . .

"You don't get us one at a time. Because we
don't take turns."

millie

This is so weird.

The whole day has felt like a real crush,
even though I knew it was fake. Because this
afternoon was like reliving my entire teens: Embarrassing. Dramatic. And I can't wait to do it all over again
tomorrow.

I tried so hard not to overreact to every touch. Not
because it was awkward. Because it wasn't. Being with
them all day actually felt really natural. It was the whole
I-kept-getting-wet part that had me in a chokehold.

And I don't mean by the ocean.

Although, I did almost drown when TJ grabbed me
and threw me in, simply because I kept holding on to
him. I'm pretty sure I bordered on pervy.

I can't help it. Every time I look at him, I keep thinking
about the almost kiss in the lobby. God, his lips are so
inviting.

The bottom one even glistened because he'd licked it.

"Very thoughtful," I whisper to myself, mascara wand suspended in the air.

I take a deep breath, laughing to myself as I remember the yang to the yin of that memory.

When we were walking back to the hotel from the beach, our eyes connected for a long moment, and I panicked again. However, I'm super grateful that when I spun around right into that palm tree, it didn't leave a mark or impale me with a coconut.

Which, according to the signs around town, does actually happen.

What is wrong with me? I can't remember the last time I was this nerdy about kissing a guy. It has to be because when one looks, so does the other.

And it doesn't matter *why* they're looking…it just feels infinitely dirty. Which is why the sexual tension felt so thick as we walked back. I didn't know if I was hot because I was sunburned or because I was burning…to be railed.

I'm almost scared to leave the bathroom. It's been my safe haven since we got back. They even went to the gym to shower.

I roll my shoulders, trying to relieve the tension littering my body before placing my mascara back in the tube and pumping it a few times. Immediately, I think dirty thoughts.

Oh, man.

I know I'd said, "Let's get to know each other," but damn. *Just, damn.* First off, the chemistry is undeniable. And I'm starting to think maybe Eleanor has a point. Who says I can't get revenge and laid? Not me. *Maybe not me?*

Could I actually fuck both of them…together? Probably not, because I might kill myself falling off the bed or something since I can't even manage to kiss one of them without losing control of my body.

I pause again, mid-mascara-stroke, staring at myself.

What if this is just an act? Like, they're laying it on thick to make me more comfortable because I'm acting like an Amish virgin.

Somebody order a butter churn on Amazon stat.

No...no way. They'd deserve Oscars, BAFTAs, People's Choice Awards.

They were definitely my down-below slutty person's choice award winners.

There's zero chance they're faking. *Hmmm.* God, this is such a mindfuck. This is exactly why the people on *The Bachelor* are crying and body-slamming tables on week two.

Fake can feel way too real when you're pretending.

The thought makes me tap my lip gloss against the vanity counter.

Doesn't matter, though, because the play that is literally about us isn't finished...there's more pretending to be had. We have the last act before we can expect our standing O.

I smile because these dirty jokes just keep presenting themselves.

Still...we have to kiss. No way we sell this tonight if we don't.

Just thinking about it has my stomach turning into a butterfly mosh pit. They're flapping around in there, hitting each other and the walls.

We're collectively panicking.

A soft knock on the bathroom door calls my attention.

"You done yet, Smalls?"

"Yeah, just about. Two minutes."

Another deep breath expands my chest as I put the final touches on myself.

"Okay. There's no turning back now," I whisper.

I rub my lips together, still in disbelief I'm actually wearing this skirt (*tube top*), before I square my shoulders and open the bathroom door.

Both sets of eyes lift at the same time from where they're sitting side by side on the bed. There's an internal squeal, but I'm ignoring it. I'm maintaining.

"Well." I exhale. "You saw me try this on over jean shorts and a tank top. So, this should be automatically better. Am I hookery enough?"

I'm standing in the strapless micro hot pink corset and low-rise black mini, accessorized with a rhinestone-studded G-string high on my hips.

For fun, I threw on the same shoes I had on the night I surprised Chad.

They're the only ones I want to walk over his grave with.

But I'm not focused on my outfit. I am, however, trying not to drool over the fact that they've both got rolled-up shirtsleeves. And Nate's thighs are comfortably snug in a pair of black slacks.

The guys stand together, dropping their phones behind them onto the bed, still unspeaking.

I almost laugh because for the first time today, *they* look like two fish out of water. Like a pair of Ricky Bobbys. And neither knows what to do with their hands.

TJ keeps almost saying words, looking at the ground and then back to my face before he gives up and shoves his hands into his pockets, settling on a smirk.

Nate's no better, just crossing and uncrossing his arms before he concedes and grips the back of his neck.

I've rendered them speechless.

I bite my bottom lip just as Nate circles his finger, demanding a spin. *Who am I to deny him?* I slowly tiptoe around in my heels.

"If it's an L, I don't want to know because we're never finding another outfit this late in the game."

"It's a dub, baby."

The smile on my face blooms even further as I stop in front of them, unable to stop myself from what I'm about to say.

"Oh, come on," I tease. "What are you trying to say? Are you trying to tell me you think I'm superhot? Like, can't-take-your-eyes-off-me hot? How long have you felt this way? Honestly, I'm a little offended. I'm more than my body."

They both smirk, but their eyes roam. Oh shit. *When one looks, so does the other.* Something changes as I stand there. It's a familiar charge that seems to course through my veins, leaving goose bumps in its wake.

I let out a small exhale, running my hands over my waist. And I swear I can hear my own breath, feel my pulse strumming.

This is the moment. Band-Aid. Rip.

"So I was thinking—" I start but get interrupted.

"I know we're making him jealous—" Nate's voice rumbles like fresh gravel on the road as he steps to me, takes my hand, and brings it to his lips. "—but you look like I'm gonna end up in jail."

He brushes a kiss over my knuckles, lingering.

Oh fuck. I got this. I can do this. Instead of saying anything though, I just lick my lips, trying to prepare as he presses another to the top of my hand.

TJ strides closer, pulling my focus. I can feel my chest

starting to rise faster. My senses are immediately overwhelmed and sharp all at once.

"Smalls, you could drive a good man bad."

I shiver as he winds a finger around a strand of my hair, leaning down and inhaling. Holy shit. A quiet breath tickles my parted lips.

This is exactly what they've done to me all afternoon. Sandwiched me between them. I don't even think they know they do it. It's just their raw nature.

Okay. Say it. Say it now.

I blink, trying to focus, feeling dizzy in the best way but still needing some space. My palms find hard chests, attempting to push them back, but all I get is the pressure of immovable muscle.

Oh, this is fucking with my brain chemistry.

"Here's the thing," I whisper, feeling almost intoxicated by their closeness. Nate's tight jaw matches TJ's as they stare down at me. "I think we're comfortable. We've accomplished getting past the first-date vibes."

They instantly step away as if I've yelled "cut" to our homemade porn, misunderstanding me.

I slide my hands down their torsos, stopping in the one place I shouldn't be.

Curled around leather belts, my fingers dip just inside the waistbands of their black slacks. As if that wasn't the worst part, my fingers have slipped in between the fabric of one of their shirts, and I'm touching warm skin. *I hope.*

Whose...I have no idea because my mind is mush. *Oh. My. God.*

"Sorry," I rush out, but I don't move.

Why aren't I moving. What is wrong with me.

My eyes are fixed on them, shifting between their belts.

I'm glitching. This is the Matrix. Except instead of a red or blue pill, I have to decide between Nate or TJ. That's the fundamental flaw, Neo—why choose?

Fuck. Let go, weirdo. You're holding for too long.

"Sorry," I say again, my mind finally catching up.

But as I retreat, letting Nate go, TJ circles my wrist, holding my hand where it is, still just barely tucked inside.

He's the flesh.

"Are you...sorry?"

We're locked on each other, and the room suddenly feels quieter. Smaller. Like the walls have closed in around us so they can eavesdrop on the sound of my heart.

I press my lips together, not answering. Except I do, because I shake my head.

Oh my god. What am I doing?

TJ's fingers start at my elbow, and immediately, the memory of him drawing on my stomach springs to mind. He scorches a line down my arm, ghosting his touch over my skin until he reaches the top of my hand.

I'm watching, eyes dropped to my hand. Knowing... feeling Nate watch, too, just as TJ turns his fingers and joins mine, forcing my hand just a bit deeper.

My breath stutters, but TJ's voice is deep and quiet, rattling my bones.

"Someone's being a bad girl and breaking the rules." He clucks his tongue. "You said we'd stay above the waist, perv."

He presses his lower abdomen forward in the smallest, almost immeasurable way before dragging my hand out from below his belt and letting me go.

But I feel him. Everywhere. I suck in a quiet breath, changing my attention between them.

"What are we doing?" It comes out breathless and barely a whisper.

Two sets of eyes, one hazel, one brown, are narrowed and bored into me. Their defined jaws are slack, muscular bodies unmoving, as if they're waiting for the word to eat me alive.

Fuck, I'd swallow, but right now, I think that might give them the wrong idea. Or maybe the right one. I clasp my hands behind my back, making my tits jut forward as I lick my lips again.

"What do you want to do?" Nate growls, and it makes my eyes slow blink.

"Maybe we should—"

"Kiss," TJ finishes. I immediately nod.

TJ hums, sliding his fingers down my arms until he reaches my hands, tugging them apart. "I like hands in my hair," he whispers with gravel in his tone.

Oh shit. It's happening. This is happening. Michael Scott, get out of my head. I'm too horny.

TJ leans down, closing in on my lips, sending my pulse through the roof. So, I close my eyes and lift my chin, finally ready, until a hard thud bounces off his chest.

Stopping him in place.

He lets out a hard exhale before producing a grunt as he's moved backward. "Dude, you can't hit that hard when I don't have pads on."

My eyes turn owllike before Nate's other hand drifts up my neck, his fingers firmly woven into the hair at my nape as he steps in between us.

I am so out of my league.

"Get off my girlfriend."

73

TJ chuckles as Nate's eyes lock on mine, his lips already parted as he tugs me forward, dragging my body to his. No hesitation, no pause, nothing said.

All. Hot.

I barely get my tongue swiped over my lip before his mouth seals over mine, rough and dominant. Fuck. He's hungry and warm, growling into my lips. His tongue dips inside without permission or invitation, owning me and making my knees weak.

He kisses exactly like he is—controlled, intense, and powerful.

Nate takes from me.

Our mouths open and close, our heads tilting one way and then the other. I whimper into his mouth, pressing against him as his hand tightens in my hair and my palms run over his pecs.

Nate's kissing the fuck out of me, but I feel my waist being pawed.

A strong set of hands grips my sides before I'm stolen. My pulse is racing, my eyes barely able to complete a full blink, even as Nate tries holding my bottom lip between his teeth.

It glides out as I hear from the other side of me, "Uh-uh. That's enough." I'm spun around as a rough hand grips my jaw, lifting my chin and wiping a thumb under my lip to clean up the mess.

"I like your mouth like this."

Fuck.

Dark pupils set inside green eyes with amber flecks flirt with me before looking past my eyes directly at my mouth. TJ smirks before lowering his hand and closing around my throat.

His lips hover over mine, and I swallow, hyperaware

of where his hand is. For a moment, I think he might push my head back further and kiss my jaw.

I wouldn't stop him.

But he doesn't. He presses his mouth to mine roughly before pulling back. Like he's sampling me.

I open my eyes, feeling like I'm waking from a dream.

TJ licks his lips. "Just a taste before the meal." Before I even take a breath, both of his palms cradle my face, and the hell is kissed out of me. Again.

Holy shit, he knows what he's doing.

His tongue flirts and teases, charming a moan from me. He nips my bottom lip before sucking on it gently and diving back in. Jesus, every dip of his tongue feels like edging until he lays a full kiss on me.

"Hands," he growls, and I obey instantly, weaving my fingers through his hair.

TJ groans loudly before pulling away, keeping his eyes on mine. His jaw is slack, and he's as breathless as I am, but his hand lowers, palm pressing to the top of my chest as I'm forced to take half a step back.

Directly into a massive hard chest.

Nate.

"Back where you belong, Smalls."

Oh shit. I'm completely gone. Lost in this moment. Untethered.

Floating around in the Nate and TJ universe.

TJ turns me around so that I'm facing Nate, my body now pressed between them.

"Do we need to kiss again?" I whisper as my palms rest on Nate's chest.

He nods before looking over my head for a beat, then back at me. "Yeah, baby. But this time, you need to kiss us like you're *ours*."

"Yours—"

The only answer is his mouth on mine. There's not even room for debate. I melt into him as different hands come to my waist. TJ's rich, deep voice tickles my ear.

"You don't get us one at a time. Because we don't take turns."

His lips skim the delicate spot under my ear as he kisses my neck. It's soft, needy, and wet. And I moan. Unabashedly.

Without warning, my chin is pulled, and TJ's tongue dives inside my mouth as Nate's lips wet my throat.

Jesus, I've never felt so innately sexual and sexualized. It feels like being fucked. But all our clothes are on.

In the distance, I hear my ringtone, but I don't care. I'm lost in lips and big hands running over my body and up my sides.

Nate's tongue runs over my clavicle, and my clit throbs. I grip someone's shirt, trying to press my body closer to both of theirs.

"Millie."

"Yes," I whisper back, but my eyes spring open just as TJ's teeth scrape my jaw.

That wasn't them.

"Mills. Millie Boobie Brown."

Oh my god. Eleanor. She's in our living room. *How'd she get a key?*

I bat at them before I jerk away, adrenaline making me sharp again. The guys each reach for me like animals, but Eleanor runs her mouth again, sobering everyone up.

"Millie. I know you hear me. This room is seven square feet. Chad's a dick. P.S. If you're having sex...tell the Tweedles to wrap it up. Car's downstairs. And next time, answer your phone, whore."

Nate grins, using his finger to wipe our spit from around his lips as he kisses my cheek. "You heard your friend. She wants us to wrap it up. I'll go out and let her know we got plenty in the drawer by the bed."

My mouth falls open as he turns and heads toward the door. But Elle yells again, making me laugh. She's such an asshole. And I'm in over my head.

"Hurry up. I can hear you in there. It's gross."

I screech back, still trying to process what just *almost* happened. "I'm coming."

TJ kisses my other cheek, whispering into it, "Not yet."

He heads toward the door, too, as I gawk. Nate opens it, leaving me standing in my place, blushing like all hell.

Eleanor locks eyes with me and laughs.

"Ummm…Mills Valley, you got a smudge right here." She motions around her whole face. "Might wanna fix that up again."

Oh my god. Nate, TJ, Chad, this moment…None of it was on my goddamn bingo card for this year. I walk to the door and shut it before getting myself re-ready for what feels like the longest, horniest night of my life.

eleven

. . .

"Show me what you got, girlie."

nate

Do not get hard. Do not. Get hard.

This is pretend. She's putting on an act. That's it. That's all.

I keep repeating that statement in my head over and over, but it's not helping because our little Scrappy Doo has been grinding her ass into my dick for the last hour to rap music like she wants to get pregnant.

"Get a room," Eleanor yells over the music, making Millie laugh as she and Crew leave to go to the bar.

Fuck me, don't say room. If I thought not fucking her in the hotel was hard, I was wrong. This is worse. What I do know for sure is that fake boyfriend is feeling a lot like being a real one.

Because since the minute she walked into this club, doing her best to make Chad reevaluate his whole life, he hasn't taken his eyes off her.

It was exactly the plan. I should be thrilled.

Tonight was for driving him crazy and really driving home the cleat chaser comment until he hated life. Bonus points if we make him so mad that he tries to talk to her... regardless of his girl.

But I don't like it.

This is because I got a taste. Goddammit. That kiss got out of my control.

And that's fucking with my head.

Real bad, because currently, all I want is to make him take his eyes *off* her. Maybe leave both his fucking eyes so swollen that he can't even picture his memory of her in the goddamn dark.

Why couldn't she have been a shitty kisser? Or have a little less "fuck me" in those pretty eyes of hers?

I run my hand through my hair with my other on her hip, trying like hell to guide her ass away from my cock while she dances and kisses TJ.

She's doing that a lot. Kissing him.

My eyes narrow as I watch.

What is wrong with me? What the fuck do I care?

Get it together, you idiot. We're supposed to be sharing her.

It's like the minute our mouths touched, all the blood went the wrong way.

All the irrational thoughts keep saying, *I don't share the girls I date.* But logic keeps shouting, *You're not fucking dating her for real.*

Either way, I've never wanted a chick between me and TJ more. Especially since she took to it like a fucking pro. The way she melted into me and followed our lead—fuck.

Do not. Get hard.

I'm never making it out alive this week. Fuck that. I may not make it out tonight. There's nothing worse than a club.

Everyone's sweaty, bobbing to the music, grinding in the dark. It's the perfect recipe for debauchery to ensue. And the kind of dirty shit I want to do to her.

Millie's hand grips the fabric on my thigh as she leans into me, the back of her head on my chest. A growl rumbles my body because her eyes are closed and she's licking her lips.

Jesus, she's so fucking sexy. So vulnerable, without a shred of caution whispering in her ear despite how nervous she was earlier today.

I want to run my hand down her chest and splay my fingers over her stomach, anchoring her in place for TJ to—

My dirty thoughts are interrupted because she opens her eyes, batting those long lashes up at me. I smirk and lower my head, kissing the tip of her nose gently. Millie wraps an arm around my neck, calling up to me.

"Drink?"

I nod, so she lifts the cup she's holding in her free hand over her head to my lips before tipping it back. The booze hits hard, but I laugh as she pulls it away. Since she's upside down, some of the liquid spills down my jaw.

I lift my hand to wipe it, but Millie beats me to it, spinning around and pulling me closer. Her fingers weave into my hair before she licks up my neck like a goddamn animal.

Oh. Fuck.

My eyes instantly close, my fingers digging into her flesh, strained around the bejeweled strings of her panties. I fucking love when girls kiss my neck.

"All clean," she rasps.

This girl is testing everything I got.

My jaw's tense enough to break my damn teeth. I can't even open my eyes because I swear to god, if she's giving me that look like before, I will fuck her on this dance floor.

And let that dickhead ex of hers watch how it's supposed to be done. I'll put the fucking mic right to her lips so he doesn't miss her screaming my name.

TJ's voice cuts in, so I know he closed in behind her just as the song changed. Or maybe it didn't change. I don't know. All the blood is going the wrong fucking way again.

"DJ douche is watching us like a hawk. He hasn't even looked at Moondust, who's wildin' out with those glow sticks. Maybe it's your time to shine, Nate."

He knows that girl's name is Moonbeam, but he'll never say it right.

Just for Mills.

I open my eyes, about to make an excuse not to leave right where I am. But as I do, Millie turns her head and looks toward the DJ booth on the stage. Right where Chad's been hanging.

And it pisses me off. *I'm not done with her.*

"Eyes on me," I bark. Millie's face whips back, eyes sparkling, a small smile grabbing at the corners of her mouth. "Good girl."

She holds her drink up as her other hand blazes a trail up my chest and clasps around my neck. The three of us begin moving our bodies to the music rhythmically. Sexually. And it's not even on purpose. It just is what it is.

Still, her eyes never leave mine as the bass vibrates in heavy drops.

Millie lazes back against TJ's chest, her hand still clasped around my neck, making her tits bounce with

81

each move. But my gaze drops to the dip at the bottom of her throat, suddenly wishing I could taste the glisten.

I shift, letting my thigh slip between hers, needing her closer. Just enough so we can press her against us, me in the front, TJ in the back, seamlessly.

My hands roam her slick back as TJ glides up her rib cage, forcing her arms in the air. His hands intertwine with hers, even around the drink.

"Show me what you got, girlie," TJ rumbles, making her smile and grind harder between us.

Jesus, this is making me fucking crazy.

Fuck it. Show us, baby.

I hook a finger just under that strap of her G-string again, drawing it up with every movement, knowing she can feel the friction right where it counts.

She sucks in a breath, eyes closed. Her head sways with the music as she grinds in rhythm. *You're fucking perfect.*

I feel wild. The fucking thoughts I'm having aren't just hedonistic.

They're possessive and visceral. I want Millie to ride my fucking thigh until her body quivers.

Just so I can kneel at her feet and clean her cum off her thighs.

With my fucking tongue.

Her chest's rising and falling, heaving even faster when TJ gathers her hair and lifts, blowing on the back of her neck. She shivers, so I tug that damn string higher, making her eyes flutter.

The song changes again, all the bass silenced before some EDM bullshit starts to thump.

It's almost as if somebody wanted to pour cold water on us.

TJ smirks before we both glance at the booth. Chad's speaking with his hands, real animated, to a security guard.

Millie straightens, garnering our attention. Her head shifts toward the DJ booth, a frown on her face.

TJ motions to me with a shrug, but I shake my head because I don't know what's going on either.

What I do know is that she's slipped her hand into mine just like she did in the elevator when seeing Chad made her feel some kind of way.

"What's wrong?" I bellow above the music.

She swallows, not looking up at me. So, I bend closer.

"I said, what's wrong, Scrappy."

Her hand cups around my ear as she lifts her chin. My jaw tenses, listening to her tell me that the house song now playing was the song Chad first played for her when they met.

He'd told her it was *her* mix.

I'd like to be happier about this, but she's bothered. So, I'm pissed. I shift my attention to the booth, where Chad's staring down. Actually, not staring down anymore...he's making his way toward us.

Here we fucking go.

I stand to my full height and squeeze her hand before motioning to Crew and Eleanor that we're leaving. Not that they're paying attention to anything but each other's tongues.

Chad closes in on us, calling her name as he pushes through the people dancing. "Millie...Millie...I just want to talk to you..."

I pull her close into my side, shaking my head, eyes locked to my best friend.

"Not even close to her, Teej."

It's the only warning I need to give. All the money I have says he'll take care of it.

As I start to lead her away, TJ winks and slips the plastic cup out of her hand, making her arm outstretch as she looks over her shoulder.

"Wait—" she rushes out, halting us before her hand covers her mouth, trying to hide her burst of laughter.

Because TJ's shoved the cup right through that dick's sternum with a "Hold this. Thanks."

Chad's mouth hangs open as he stands in the middle of the club, all the wind knocked out of him, so much so that he can't move as he holds the mangled plastic cup, and Millie's paloma drips down his stupid fucking shirt.

I smirk as TJ puts his hands on her waist, turning her around so I can lead us straight out of the club.

Me at her twelve. TJ at her six.

The only thought left circling feels like a real big complication.

Why does this feel exactly like where she belongs?

twelve

. . .

"And...RIP me."

millie

The minute we got out of the club, I screamed and high-fived them.

Then I kissed them... *Both* of them.

Right smack on the lips.

And somehow, in that moment, even though we'd just been acting out a live-action Sodom and Gomorrah, I felt shy. Embarrassed.

But that's the funny thing about dark places. Like inside of a club or a bedroom...they're not the same vibe as a well-lit sidewalk with tourists all around.

There's something about random dudes in Tevas wearing a puka shell necklace, asking if we know a good place for poi, that really rains down *presence* on your sexual fog.

Still though, there was no hiding the flush on my body or the silent recognition that whatever had started in the bedroom carried over into that club.

And as if to highlight that point, the whole way home, from the back of the car to the hotel hall, we wore barely hidden smiles that only grew bigger every time we made eye contact.

I let out a whoosh of air, still juiced up with adrenaline, still thinking about the entire night while tapping my fingers on my stomach. I've been lying here, staring at the ceiling of the hotel room, ever since we got back.

There's a lot to unpack. For starters, I have a sex crush on the Tweedles... Actually, the bags are light. That's the only one. The only thought.

I want them. On me. All over me. *Inside me.*

Eleanor said it best: "Do them both, then your heart's safe." Jumping their bones has zero downside. Plus, it's not like I'd become so fanatic for dick that I'd fall in love in a week, anyway.

Who does that?

I kick at the blanket, pulling one leg out as I lie sprawled out on the king bed. *What if I go out there and invite them in?*

No, that's so weird. Like, hey, wanna come bang me? My eyes tick to the door, complete darkness surrounding the cracks in the jamb. They're already sleeping.

Of course, they are. We had a big night. And tomorrow's another big mission.

Still, a thought niggles. The entirety of it has to do with how good they must be in bed because I just thought the word *big* twice.

Two bigs...big dick energy...Nate and TJ...Nate's and TJ's big dicks.

Oh my god. I'm out of control. But they're just so yummy.

I wonder what star signs they are?

I bet TJ's a Leo. Because he loves being in the spotlight. And I bet Nate's a Scorpio...Scorpio men are not to be fucked with. He was so dominant leading me out of that club, his broad, muscular shoulders cutting through the sea of people without having to slow.

I free my other leg from under the cover, suddenly feeling hotter, before nabbing my phone off the nightstand to look at my astrological app.

I'm scrolling, looking for what our sexual compatibility is, as another thought bubbles. This time, my eyes close, and with it, I remember how Nate pulled on my G-string. It was entitled. Like he owned my pussy.

Shit. I definitely don't need an app to tell me that my *vag*...I mean, Sag...that my Sagittarius likes his Scorpio and his friend's Leo.

I chuckle to myself because I've literally developed a one-track mind. Sleep...I just need to sleep, and tomorrow, we can just see where it goes. I'll throw out some signals, let them know I'm interested.

Perfect. *Kind of.*

In theory, that makes sense, but in application, there's no way it's working. I'm not getting to sleep anytime soon. Not unless I run a mile just to blow off steam.

I'm all wound up like the toy I wish they were playing with.

My tongue darts out, wetting my lips as a mischievous smile blooms. *There are other ways to blow off steam.*

The tickle of my fingertips along my lower stomach is all the consent my body needs. My clit instantly throbs, aching to be touched. It's the physical representation of *Yes, Queen, finally.*

Never has anyone needed to come more than me.

I'm feral. Nate and TJ were so dominant and intense

tonight. The way they moved on the dance floor was molten. Every touch felt too soaked in insinuation, and if TJ nipped at my lips one more time, I was going to melt.

Oh god.

My hand drifts down over the band of my panties before I crane my neck, eyes on the door, ensuring darkness from under it. *Perfect.*

I quickly snuggle under the covers, chuckling to myself as I pull them over my head and dive my hand directly inside my underwear.

"Oh fuck," I whisper.

The tension in my body contracts deeper, making my legs squeeze together as I rub, enjoying that first hit.

Thoughts of the night, their muscular bodies, and that damn practice kiss infiltrate my senses until I'm steadily circling my finger over my clit.

I'm so slick I didn't even need to lick them. *Damn.*

It's because I'm wet with lust.

Arching my back, I only slightly spread my legs, thinking about the way TJ would probably grip and force them open before sinking inside me. He'd start slow before punishing my pussy, making me beg to come.

"Yes," I say on a husky exhale.

My hips meet my rhythm, pressing into the feel of my finger, all my breath beginning to become stuttered. I raise my knee, wanting more, wishing I could feel them inside of me. I imagine being rolled to the side, leg swung over Nate's hip as TJ rims my ass. Nate's head at my pussy before the warmth of my body envelops their hard cocks, making room for them. Accepting the fullness. All the nerves welcoming the spark and friction of being fucked by two men at the same time.

I fuck myself faster as the scene changes in my mind.

TJ's head between my thighs, devouring my taste. Licking me, tonguing my cunt. Eating me, his arms hooked around my thighs, not letting me go as I squirm.

"TJ," I rasp. "It's so good."

My body undulates as my finger and arm move even faster. The delicious build climbs higher and higher, almost painful, into that desire to get to the moment of earth-shattering bliss.

My mind is sexually combusting. Thoughts splinter into images, getting dirtier and dirtier.

Me on my back with Nate's cock in my mouth.

Bent over with TJ in my ass.

Them jerking off over me.

TJ's cock in my mouth with Nate's hand on the back of my head.

"Oh god. Yes. Yes. Yes…Nate…TJ—"

I throw the blanket off, all my fantasies exploding like fireworks as my stomach contracts, lifting my head off the bed, and I come hard.

"*Oh my god*," comes out as a scream.

Pleasure has officially met panic.

Because I'm staring directly into TJ Knox's and Nate DeLuca's eyes.

My whole body's still quivering as I scramble, flopping around in the bed, covering myself completely. I'm not wholly convinced whether I'm getting up or hiding forever.

Hiding forever. That's the only correct answer.

They heard me…they saw.

Dear god, please let that have been a horny hallucination.

Like I came so hard that maybe a tiny blood vessel popped and I manifested my thoughts into unreal, real people.

Heavy breaths leave my chest as I root around in the darkness before peeking my head out from under the covers, sucking in the cooler air as I come free, knowing exactly what I'm going to see.

"I...I—" I don't even know what to say.

Because they're like gods. Standing in the moonlight. Shirtless in boxer briefs. A set of chiseled features that call for depravity and filth. And they're looking at me like if I said the word, they'd flip me over and fuck me raw.

Maybe that's wishful thinking?

"We knocked," Nate levels like he's dumbstruck, opening and closing his mouth like a fish.

I wish he was because then I'd be drowning and never have to live through this moment. My eyebrows couldn't get any higher as my silence remains the only thing I have to offer.

This isn't happening. I'm screaming in my head. Oh my god.

OH. MY. GOD.

TJ smirks, biting his bottom lip before he points to the bathroom. "We just needed—"

My head nods too fast, and it won't stop. *Fucking stop already.*

"Yeah. Sure. Yep. Whatever you need. I'm just soo tired. So tired." I fake yawn, attempting to sell it. It doesn't. And even though, on the inside, I can't believe my mouth is still fucking moving, more words keep coming out. "I mean...not *because* of any reason." I laugh awkwardly, but they just stand there smirking those fucking smirks. "You know, just because long night. Because yeah...I'm going to sleep. Immediately. Narcileptically."

I jerk the blanket back over my head, silently

screaming with my mouth wide open, listening to the footsteps. I'm bright damn red, I know it. I can feel the heat from my neck to my face. I literally just came, saying their names, to their faces.

If I was a hotter version of myself, I would've thrown the blanket back and rang the dinner bell. *Come and get it, boys.*

But like, oh my god. *Why. Why me?*

I'm chewing the inside of my cheek and trying not to laugh under the blanket before my hand sneaks out, patting the nightstand and snatching my phone inside.

Eleanor better be up because this is one of those moments in life you have to share. Like when you see a video of a cat stepping on tinfoil.

These moments are canon.

> Me: They caught me "self-caring"
>
> Me: ELEANOR ROOSEVELT
>
> Me: I fucking came, toes curled, Kim K's ugly cry face on as they walked in. AND LOCKED EYES WITH ME.

> Elle: HAHAHAHAHAHAHAHA-HAHAHAHA
>
> Elle: So I take it you guys haven't yet?

> Me: No!!!!!! Jesus, we've been here for two days.

And we're fake dating. But that's for another day.

Elle: Puhleessse, bitch. Once you fuck them, you're gonna be pissed you only have eight days left. Just sayin'. What are you waiting for?

My personality to completely change and give me the nerve to proposition them.

Me: Ewww, stop Yelp reviewing them. I can never leave this room. So I'm waiting for forever. I'll die here. This text is my last will and testament. You get my jewelry.

Elle: You shop at Claire's. Listen ... Just invite them in...like vampires. Except YOU suck them dry.

Me: I hate you.

Elle: *kiss

Why did I even tell her? But I can't help myself. I giggle—too loudly—giving myself away because before the bedroom door closes again, I hear, "Sweet dreams, girlie. Just make sure they're about me...again."

And...RIP me.

thirteen

· · ·

"I paid to watch something like this on pay-per-view at a motel once."

tj

She still hasn't come out of that room.

I can't help but smile to myself on this goddamn uncomfortable cot. We slept, the sun rose, our wake-up call came, but Millie...she's been quiet as a mouse.

It's understandable. Last night almost made me lose my damn mind.

The way she stared right into my eyes after saying my name made me want to drag her off that bed and flip her over so we could start her up again.

Fuck, just knowing there was cum on her fingers.
Goddamn.

I swear I was two seconds from walking to the side of her bed, grabbing her hand out, and cleaning those suckers off.

But I couldn't do that. Because if she'd wanted me there...*or us,* she would've asked.

93

So now we're doomed to know that we only get to fuck her in her dreams. Which means a whole week of blue balls.

I shift my head to look at Nate, laughing again because he's fallen back to sleep. He looks like a giant baby in that chair, cradled up with his hairy-ass legs draped over the side.

The remote in my hand is already in the air, hurdling toward him, hitting right smack on his shoulder.

"Fuck," he groans, opening his eyes and sitting up with his hands in front of his face for protection, half-dazed. "Stop." I laugh, and he stretches before motioning toward the door. "She peek out yet?"

I shake my head with a yawn.

"On a scale of one to ten, how awkward is today gonna be?"

"Fifty-seven," I answer, grinning again. "Fuck it. We gotta rip the Band-Aid, Nathan."

"Why are you calling me by my real name?"

I ignore him, craning toward the door. "Mills..." No answer. "Millie, are you awake?" Her footsteps sound just before the lock clicks on the door. "Smalls, come on. We got spa day revenge today. And then there's surfing tomorrow...the luau alone is enough to suck it up and come out for."

Damn. She's really trying to rot in there. I reach for my phone, winking at Nate and making a clicking sound with my tongue between my teeth.

He frowns. "Why do you look like that? What are you doing?" I don't answer him as my fingers fly over the keyboard. "TJ...Teej. Nothing about the look on your face is making me feel good right now."

The ding on his phone is my only answer as I look up, smiling ear to ear.

"Ahh...I already know it's dumb," he groans, head falling back before he grabs his phone off the coffee table and swipes it open.

> Me: Mornin' Smalls. We were just wondering if you were ever coming out or if maybe your wrist was too sore to turn the handle?

"Noooo...Teej. Why?" Nate chuckles, running his hand through his hair, entertained and fearful all at once.

"Look at the group name."

His eyes drop, then dart back to mine. *"Shit you can only say in the dark*...really?"

I shrug, adjusting my head on Freddie. "You got a better idea?" His brows rise in thought, but I continue. "She's gotta get over it, dude. It's natural. It happens. And sometimes the best way to say shit is when you can't see other people looking at you."

He shakes his head. "You're fucking dumb. She's never gonna speak to us again." He grins. "Or maybe just you...she did say my name first last night."

I scoff-laugh. "Well, the saying is *'save the best for last.'* So..."

A ding lowers both our heads.

> Millie: I can hear you.

Nate and I lock eyes before we laugh, loud.

"Millie, get out here," I yell again.

> **Millie:** Sorry. No can do. Who even is this? I don't know anyone here in Hawaii. Especially guys named Nathan and TJ. This you, Elle? Did you get a new phone?

> **Me:** Stop being embarrassed. I jerk off all the time when Nate's in the other room.

The remote I threw at him hits me now. Way harder.

"Oww," I grind out, chuckling after. "You're so aggressive."

> **Nate:** Millie... If you don't come out here, I might kill him. Because he's bound to say something that deserves it.

> **Millie:** If I come out... You are not allowed to make any jokes. And we are pretending nothing happened. At all.

> **Me:** K...but last one...who was better?

> **Millie:** TJ!!!!!!!!!

I would laugh at her yelling via text, but I'm suddenly too busy trying to avoid the violence from the asshole defensive lineman who's chasing me around the three-square-foot living room.

"Gimme the phone TJ," he grits out between his teeth, lunging for me, but I jump over the couch, still trying to text and failing as he bellows, "TJ, gimme the fucking phone."

"Millie," I shout, trying to hold on to the phone just as he puts me in a damn headlock.

"Fucker," is all I breathe out before the door clicks and opens.

We freeze, eyes locked on her.

Two shirtless assholes in our boxer briefs. Me bent over, still holding the phone just out of Nate's reach as his bicep chokes me to death.

She's backlit by the morning sun, standing in her underwear and tank, her hair in my favorite version of a messy bun as she smiles at us.

Millie leans a shoulder against the jamb, crossing her arms and chewing on her thumbnail before her tongue darts out over her lips.

She motions toward us. "I paid to watch something like this on pay-per-view at a motel once. It was hot." She hitches the nibbled-on thumb over her shoulder. "The bathroom's yours if you need it."

Okay. Nate lets go of me, so I stand. We both clear our throats, trying not to smile, resetting like she asked.

I walk toward her, only pausing to gently kiss her cheek before I pass by and act like nothing ever happened.

"You want some coffee?" Nate offers, and I hear her say, "Yeah. Sounds good."

But you know what else sounds good, Mills?

You.

fourteen

. . .

"Are we committing shhmurrder, Smalls?"

millie

"Hi, checking in for the half-day rejuvenation packages. DeLuca, Knox, and Dwyer."

A sweet and really pretty redhead at the front desk smiles and clicks the keys as I look over my shoulder, knowing Chad and Moonbeam will arrive shortly.

Nate stretches next to me, calling my eyes. But before I can full-on gawk, I look forward again. I may be pretending nothing happened, but every time I look at either of them, I have to actively work at not smiling.

If they only knew the filthy shit I let them do in my mind. Well, they kind of do know since I was moaning their names like I was auditioning for Pornhub. Jesus.

Maybe I should text them in the dark.

The thought makes me grin. I can't lie, TJ's group text was a good idea because I was starting to think of ways to scale the building just so I didn't have to look them in the eyes.

"Okay," the clerk says, smiling and tugging me back into the present. "You're all checked in. May I offer any of you water or tea?"

I shake my head, not letting the boys even answer. "No, thank you. But I was hoping you could help me with something else. My boyfriend is coming down in a few minutes—" TJ scoffs, so I kick him. "He'll be down with his sister. His name is Chad Stevens."

Her brows draw together as she looks at the schedule. "Oh yes, with a Miss…"

"Moonwalk," TJ teases, actually doing it, sliding away like he should be wearing a sparkly glove on one hand, making me laugh before I turn back to her.

I need him to stop being so cute. It's ruining my life. And I swear he's being even more flirty. Or maybe I'm in a sexual tidal wave. Where there's no escaping, so I'll just drown in my horniness.

"*Beam*…Moonbeam. Sorry, he's an idiot." TJ raises his eyebrows before I feel him try and pinch my ass, but I swat his hand, ignoring him. Fuck me. "Anyway, I was hoping to do something special for Chad. I booked him for the mud bath."

She nods, smiling and batting her lashes at TJ, then Nate.

I know. They're hot. You'll get over it.

But she doesn't. This little ginger vixen tucks her hair behind her ear and smiles all shy.

Okay. Easy, Amy Adams. I was literally just fucking them.

It may have all been in my mind, but that's gonna count.

I tilt my head, my nails making a strumming sound on the counter, grabbing her attention again.

"Hi. Yeah, I was saying I'd like to upgrade it to add seaweed with the mud. And maybe flowers, too, for like the vibe. It's all mixed in, right?"

She hums her answer, still staring past me. So, I look over my shoulder to where they are now. A smile breaks out when I see they're huddled together, removing the caps from all the essential oil samples and smelling them.

Oh man. They're golden retrievers. Both of them.

Nate looks up, humor plastered all over his face. "This one's triple pineapple surprise. Doesn't that sound perfect, Scrappy?"

I narrow my eyes before turning around and biting my lip. It does sound perfect...if only I could fucking get enough nerve to say that.

Red is staring at me, clearly forgetting where we left off, so I raise my brows.

"It's all mixed in? Right?"

She takes a tiny inhale, nodding. "Oh. Yes. Except the flowers. Those go just on the top for décor."

Her eyes tick toward the guys again, and on impulse, I quickly smack the counter. It's a small gesture but one that makes both our eyes widen.

Get ahold of yourself, weirdo. What am I going to do next? Walk over and pee on them to mark my territory?

We're fake dating and only imaginary fucking.

"Sorry," I chuckle, tapping the surface a few more times. "Just really feeling the music." *Now I'm into fucking woodwinds and Kenny G? Metal.* "Back to the mud bath. I'd like to surprise him. So, can that be a secret for me to reveal? He's going to be so excited that I remembered it was his favorite."

"Of course." She waves us toward the entrance. Well, not really me—to my two puppies. "Allow me to show you to the locker rooms. Your robes are waiting, and the attendants will be right with you." Her eyes lift. "Let me know if they're too small for you guys. I can try and find bigger ones."

"They'll be fine," I cut her off, still smiling as I take the lead in front of them and follow her down the quiet hallway. But the boys whisper behind me, oblivious to the offer being thrown their way.

"Mills.." ... "Millie…"

I ignore them, feeling too much body heat behind me. One in each ear.

"Revenge is usually something people don't like…" ... "Yeah, so why are we giving him flowers? And upgrading his service?"

The wily redhead turns back, and we halt. The guys straighten like there's nothing to see.

"The men's side is here." She motions left. "And the women's is just across there."

"Thank you," I breathe, waiting for her to leave before I spin around and scrunch my nose. "He's getting flowers because I like a beautiful distraction. He's getting seaweed because he has a sensitivity to it."

Nate pulls his head back to stare at me. But TJ presses his lips together before he bends, coming eye to eye with me and whispering, "Are we committing shhmurrder, Smalls?"

I giggle, pushing his face away.

"Shut up. No. He's *sensitive* to it. As in, he won't die, but he will be miserable. Think boils and rashes. All over."

My eyes drop to their crotches before I grin. "All. Over."

Nate winces, then taps my nose. "Is it too early in our fake relationship to say I might be falling in love with you?"

I wink, turning toward my locker room. "Don't be so predictable, Nathan." I spin, pressing the door open with my butt and swiping my thumb across my throat. "Everyone knows to never fall in love with the villain."

Their laughter is all I hear as the door closes behind me, and I take a deep breath. Oh man, I'm definitely in trouble. If these two get any cuter, I just may regret not taking a bite for the rest of my life.

ONE HOUR LATER, I'M RELAXED AND RUBBED DOWN, MY BODY glistening from the triple pineapple surprise I requested to be added to the oil.

The soft falls of my slippers are the only sounds in the quiet hallway as I walk back to the women's waiting area to sit before my next treatment.

A relaxed breath leaves me as I shove my hands in the big robe pockets and smile big again, remembering the interruption during my massage.

"Miss Dwyer, I am so sorry to interrupt, but there's been an incident. Your boyfriend—"

"Yes?" I smile, looking up from the massage table.

"He had a reaction to the mud bath. It was...well, they're hosing him down now. We've called the doctor. It's just that the rash is...everywhere. It's particularly hard for him to sit...or stand with his legs together."

"Well," I breathe out, settling back, "it seems you have it under control. I'm sure his sister can take care of him. He'd hate for me to see him that way."

"Okay," she says awkwardly before closing the door and leaving me to truly enjoy this bliss.

There's a spring in my step as I round the corner, still reveling in my tiny victory. My mind is deep in thought before out of nowhere, I'm assaulted.

Grabbed. And jerked into a utility closet.

"Oh my god," I barely rush out, but Nate's staring back at me, grinning down with a sucker in his mouth.

I smack his chest covered in a fluffy robe, which is indeed too small for him.

"What are you doing?"

"The news is out. My masseuse told me what happened to *your boyfriend*."

I chuckle, shimmying my shoulders, not missing how he teases the "your boyfriend" part. He tilts his head, the stick twirling between his lips.

Why is that so fucking sexy?

My eyes are fixed on it as he moves it to the other side of his mouth, and I hear the faint clinking of it against his teeth.

"Ex," I correct.

"Good," he tells me.

I can't help myself. The sucker is doing something to me. And it's because it looks like his tongue may very well be truly skilled.

Suddenly, the room feels smaller, even though the space is big enough for both of us. I start picturing him between my legs again, last night's fantasy invading my present.

Without permission, my brain goes zero dark thirty on my impulse control.

I reach up, fingers pinching the white stick, coaxing the red candy out from between his lips slowly. Silence washes over us as I watch it glide over his lips, shivering only as he lets out a quiet little slurp.

Nate steps in closer, jaw immediately slack. His breathing is heavier as he bites and tastes his bottom lip.

"Sorry," I whisper. "This looked so good. You were saying?"

No...what am I saying? What am I doing?

"I was saying that you're a mastermind, Scrappy." His eyes lock to mine before dropping back to my lips. "And I just wanted to tell you that in person."

Oh god, he's so close. And his eyelashes are so long...and his lips are...

"In the closet—" I say before I swallow, still holding the sucker between us. "—so nobody would hear us?"

My chest rises and falls, our gaze never breaking.

"Yeah." He smirks, his eyes finally ticking to the candy in my hand. "Wouldn't want to get caught doing dirty deeds."

Oh my god. Are we about to do dirty deeds? *Please?*

I feel tingly on the inside. Like that feeling you get when you haven't eaten, kind of shaky, kind of cold, but wide-awake.

A small, quiet breath passes through my lips, ripe with the tension I'm feeling.

What the hell am I doing? *Being the master of my fate... that's fucking what.* Oh shit. Who am I?

It doesn't matter what I ask myself or the pep talk I'm giving. My body has clearly denounced its relationship with my mind and is on a solo mission.

Because looking straight into eyes, saying nothing, I put his sucker in my fucking mouth, then draw it out a little to taste it...to taste *him*.

"Grape's my favorite."

Nate's hand grips my hip as he hums a deep, gravelly sound. The press of his fingers into me makes me feel slick between my thighs.

"I think you're my favorite."

I blush, biting my lip as he brings his other hand to the stick, his fingers melding over mine before he tugs. It rests on my lips before he drags the stickiness back and forth. His stare's so intense I feel it fucking everywhere.

I don't have time to say anything back because in a flash, Nate's mouth joins mine...and the sucker. His tongue swipes over it before dancing with mine as we kiss, letting the sweet taste mingle over our lips.

I'm possessed, all the lust and desire I've felt hitting me hard. My hands climb his chest, hooking around his neck as his own hit the door behind us, caging me in.

Fuck.

There's nothing slow or sensual, not romantic or flirtatious.

We're animals, clawing at each other with sloppy, desperate kisses.

The sucker hits the ground as he growls, taking my mouth again with more intensity, sealing us together in every way, and his hard body rocks into mine.

That's not all that's hard.

We're all lust, hands brushing over robed bodies, trying to push past the fluffy barriers. All our words are fumbled and muttered between our lips as we kiss like we're starved.

"I haven't stopped thinking about this since the first

time we kissed," he mutters, dropping his mouth to my jaw, nipping and licking my skin.

"Same," I exhale heavily, body buzzing and dying to be touched.

Nate growls, weaving his hand into my hair. He pulls back, staring deep into my hazy eyes.

"I fucking want you, baby. Right here. Right now."

Oh my god. This is happening. I'm breathless. Completely lost in this moment. Wanting him, but not so lost that a certain pair of hazel eyes don't pop into my head.

"Me too...what about TJ?"

His eyes stay locked on mine as I lick my lips, feeling his hand slide between my legs and past my robe before he leans closer.

"He'll get his turn. My name first means my pussy first."

I shudder, almost coming from his words, but he stills.

The look on his face is pained restraint. I watch him only half blink like he's taken a hit. I'm bare, and now he knows it.

"Millie," he groans, running his nose over my cheek slowly as I sigh, using the door as support.

My clit throbs as his fingers hover, the backs of his knuckles grazing the tender bundle of nerves.

Gasp isn't a strong enough word for what I do. Because I swear, I almost come on the spot as he dives his fingers between my slit, directly inside of me.

My hands are gripped to his shoulders, holding on as he drags them out so fucking slow. The deep bass of his voice touches me in all the right places.

"I am gonna lick you ass to clit until you're squirting in my mouth."

Oh. Fuck.

He thrusts back inside me, and I whimper, but he just smirks. Arrogant as fuck.

King.

I wind a hand around his neck to kiss him again when a loud knock bangs against my back, followed by a muffled voice.

"Excuse me. Who is in there?"

I freeze. He doesn't, forcing me to suck in another breath.

The door handle twists, and I know someone tries to open it, but Nate's big mitt isn't letting that happen.

More knocking, but his fingers move faster. My breath catches as we stare at each other, not saying a word. He's going to make me come. Right here. Right now. Just like he said.

And the whole fucking spa is going to hear it.

We can't, I mouth.

We are, he mouths back.

God, his fingers are too good. So thick inside of me. So skilled at hitting my G-spot. I lick my dry lips, my hips rocking of their own volition.

But it feels so good.

"Nate," I whisper, half plea, half protest, as my fingers dig into his shoulders.

"Millie," he whispers back, all desire.

"We shouldn't." I'm panting.

His lips touch my ear. "Then come for me. Come all over *my* hand, baby. It's only fair. You had a turn."

My mouth falls open as I hear through the door, "I'm getting security."

Shit. Footsteps stomp away, and even in my lust-filled fog, I know I have to stop this and get us both out of here.

If we get caught fucking in the closet and go to jail, TJ won't forgive us because then this throuple will remain a dream.

It takes all my strength to shake my head and push against his chest.

"Stop. Stop," I breathe.

He does immediately, stepping back, his breath heavy, eyes hooded, and his fucking fingers glistening. I swallow, searching blindly for the door handle, gripping it hard before I twist.

"We have to go to our next appointments."

Nate wipes his fingers on his robe. "I'm not tasting you until we get to fuck you. So, I guess we're both gonna be deprived until you make that call."

If I could melt into a puddle, I would.

Instead, I slip out, praying we're not caught as I rush down the hall, only looking over my shoulder once to see Nate watching me go with a grin on his face and a wink for me.

fifteen

. . .

"You gonna be a good girl? Cuz I was hoping
for a bad one."

millie

I've been lying here, my body still amped up, even
though I'm supposed to be relaxing. But something
about getting a *facial* keeps making my mind
dissolve into dirty thoughts.

The dirtiest of thoughts.

I can't believe *that* happened. One minute, I was
wondering if I'd ever get the nerve to go from self-care to
two-man aftercare, and the next, I'm being pulled into a
closet for a one-on-one.

A laugh almost escapes as my mind starts running
away because I have so many questions now.

Did he already tell TJ? What will that mean? Considering our last spa services are together...all of us...am I
supposed to be chill, like I didn't just get finger fucked
next to overly expensive products? Or will they both pick
up where Nate left off?

I smile, feeling the goop pull at my skin.

Dammit. Men.

My freaking personality can't take this kind of antici-pation. I had a small anxiety attack watching *50 First Dates*, wondering if each time she woke up would be *the* time she'd remember.

I never had this many questions about my Flaming Hot Cheetos. So, if Nate and TJ are going to act like snacks, then they need to get it together.

An appreciative hum leaves my lips, now thinking about them and Cheetos. Maybe them even eating them off me...*would that just burn or give me a UTI?*

My thoughts are graciously interrupted by the tech.

"So good, right?" the tech adds. "Your skin is loving this. This stuff is actually great for your whole body."

You know what else is good for my body...

Good god. I've turned into a depraved maniac. One kiss and I'm over here in heat, ready to give it all up for dick.

This time, I do laugh.

"Sorry, did that tickle?" She chuckles, wiping a cloth over my neck and cleaning the goop off.

I nod because there's zero chance that I'm telling her what I'm really entertained by.

With a final swipe, she lets out a sigh.

"Okay. You're all done. I'll leave you to relax, and when you're ready, the coed soaking pool is right down the hall. It's past the double doors. You'll relax there before your final service."

"Thank you," I breathe out, hearing her leave before I sit up and kick my legs over the table to stand.

I'm already chewing the inside of my cheek, trying not to smile, most definitely already blushing thinking about seeing them in the soaking pool.

Knowing I'll probably *be* soaked before I get in.

Jesus. I take a deep breath, laughing to myself as I open the door and head out.

The moment I enter the pool area, my head's swinging around, looking for them.

Okay, maybe I'm not cut out for this.

I could use a crowd right about now because my heart is pitter-pattering too damn fast. And this pestering smile I can't get rid of is a dead giveaway for what I'm thinking...which is, *I would really like you to double stuff my Oreo.*

Why do I keep thinking about food? I should've never skipped breakfast.

God, why is this place so empty? Did everyone in the damn hotel decide against doing a spa service on a Sunday afternoon?

I spy the hooks for the robes, so I make my way over and hang mine, still grinning like an idiot and thankful I changed into my bathing suit before my facial.

Because with where my head is at, I may have come out with it on fucking backward.

I just need to get into the water. Yeah, I have to relax and stop acting like someone who knows they've won the lottery but can't tell anyone.

My hand curls around the aluminum rail as I take the steps into the crystal-blue water. Little ripples form and repeat, traveling further and further away from me.

Wow. It's so warm and inviting, not cool like I'd expected.

This is heaven.

I let out a little sighed moan, standing on the second step with my eyes closed, as I enjoy the feel when I hear, "I like that sound better when you're saying my name with it."

"Ah!" I jump, squealing and losing my balance, and fall directly into the pool.

My face breaches the top of the water, my mouth opening to gasp for air like a drowned rat as I blink in the heavenly vision of TJ.

Shirtless, his perfect abs on display in short swim trunks hung low on his waist, he stands at the top of the pool stairs, smirking down at me.

"Hey, Smalls. You're all wet." *You have no idea.* I look over my shoulder for Nate, but TJ shakes his head. "He's changing. You'll get both of us soon enough."

I run my hands through my hair, trying not to read into what he just said. Except all I can think is, *Does he know, does he know, does he know?*

So, I change the subject. "You scared the shit out of me. And this pool is too shallow, I hit my tailbone on the bottom. I'm gonna sue."

He takes the steps, wading in toward me, his tongue toying with his canine.

"Want me to kiss it and make it better?"

Oof, the way he's zeroing in like I'm prey makes me want to break my own leg so I'll get caught and eaten.

I splash some water at him, feeling the heat crawl up my neck. "Shut up. Perv."

But TJ grabs me, pulling me flush against his body, making me gasp.

Oh, whoa, okay.

"Me, a perv?" The deep gravel in his voice mixed with that smirk makes every fucking part of my body pay attention. This man is far too fine. His eyes drop to my lips before coming back to mine as he adds, "*Maybe*...but I'm not the one...fucking. In. Closets."

Oh my god. Questions have been answered.

He knows.

If I was holding my breath, it just released because my mouth's fallen open. I quickly close it as he taps my nose.

I'm unable to speak, completely enamored and caught off guard all at the same time. *TJ's coming in hot.* I open my mouth again, trying to say something, but I'm nothing but a grin.

"Cat got your tongue, pussycat?"

His strong hands effortlessly glide down my thighs before guiding my legs around his waist, hooking me on.

Oh my. I swallow hard as he begins moving us through the water, with me holding on to his broad shoulders, our eyes locked, his hands comfortably palming my ass.

"Ummm," I finally eke out, hyperaware that I am dangerously close to committing yet another illegal act. "We didn't fuck."

This would be a great time for any stranger or maybe three to walk in. Again, I say, nobody staying at the Four Seasons wanted a spa appointment today.

TJ playfully narrows his eyes. "You mean you didn't come."

The feel of me and the slickness that resides there, snugged tightly against his lower stomach, is making my chest rise and fall too quickly. My back softly hits the wall of the pool as his lips hover, making me want to taste them.

He leans in slowly, running his hands up and down my bare legs, kissing me chastely before searing his words over my lips.

"How 'bout I pick up where he left off, darlin'?"

Goose bumps explode over my skin, feeling like tiny

electrical receptors creating a live-wire effect everywhere he touches me.

I'm nodding, agreeing to whatever he's saying because everything that comes out of his mouth feels like sex. *The dirty kind.*

Honestly, I think if he asked me to overthrow a corrupt third-world dictatorship with only a paperclip and a popsicle wrapper, I would blindly follow right now.

Because the filth out of his mouth is like Braveheart's speech to my pussy. And now, I just want to charge into his dick.

His lips glide over mine again, my bottom one caught between his before he pulls back. I lift my chin, chasing him, eyes barely opened.

Once they are, TJ looks at me with the sexiest fucking grin blooming like he already knows the answer to the question he's about to ask.

"Wanna see how long *we* can *not* fuck before you come?"

"Uh-huh," I breathe, caught in his spell, already panting like the fucking hussy I am.

He unhooks my legs, letting them drift to the pool floor before I'm spun around, making the water splash right as the fucking jet hits me…

Right. There.

I suck in a breath as he reaches around me before swiping my bikini bottoms to the side. He glides two fingers between my pussy and spreads it open, exposing my clit to the force of the water.

"TJ," I hiss, gripping the fucking concrete like it's a lifeline, my voice suddenly caught in my throat. "Someone could catch us."

His deep voice infiltrates my senses as he whispers in

Three Ways to Mend A Broken Heart

my ear, "You gonna be a good girl? Cuz I was hoping for a bad one."

His hard cock presses into me from behind, the heat of his defined body encapsulating me as his other arm stays firmly wrapped around my middle. My stomach contracts as I whimper in his arms, blinded by the sensation.

"Tell me something, Smalls," he growls. "Is that what you told *him*? That someone could catch you...because, baby, I'd let the world watch me fuck you. That way, everyone'd know whose pussy this is."

His dirty mouth makes me whimper, and my hips press forward. We shouldn't do this...but I really don't fucking care anymore. I was already so charged. So fucking aroused. The sweet pain of needing to come is too alluring. It's got me in a fucking chokehold.

I rock even closer to the jet, feeling his fingers knead my rib cage as his voice fills my ear again. "Atta girl. Give it what it needs."

Oh. Fuck.

TJ holds me open, my nerves hit relentlessly by that fucking stream. Pleasure ebbs and flows, gathering inside me, more and more. My nails dig into the cold, hard surface, desperate to pull me closer. The feel of that delicious sharpness beats against my clit.

"TJ. Fuck...I...please—"

His mouth finds mine, kissing me roughly, our breath equally stolen and coexisting as he draws away.

"You're so fucking pretty when you say please."

Fuck me, please. Use me, please. Make me come...please. Please. Please.

"Come on, Smalls. Use your words. I can see them on the tip of your tongue. Tell me what you want."

But I can't speak anymore, panting, circling my hips, chasing that high.

That doesn't stop TJ though.

"Do you want me inside you? Huh? Do you want me to fuck you so hard that you don't remember your name?"

My head falls back against his chest, willing his hand to run up my body and palm my breast. It's like he reads my mind.

"We could fill you if you let us. Stretch that ass while you suck my cock. Play with these tits until you're squirming and begging to come."

I'm moaning now, unabashedly, uncaring if anyone hears.

"Please," I barely say, floating on a sigh.

"Say it again."

My eyes spring open, breath catching because that wasn't TJ's voice. It was the six-foot-sexy standing in front of me, staring down, his eyes hooded as he lets his bottom lip glide out from between his teeth.

But before I can say anything, the water suddenly stops, halting my pleasure, torturously screeching it to a stop.

"What are you…" I can barely make the words come out as my head shifts, eyes trying to plead. "TJ…"

I'm blinking, so fucking turned on that I can't focus, rubbing into TJ's hand that's cupped in front of my pussy.

"Be a good girl and use your words, Millie," TJ teases, letting the water hit there before stopping it again.

My chest heaves, my mind in a whirlwind of provocative desires. I lick my lips, staring up into those chocolate-brown eyes, then dropping down Nate's body to the bulge in his pants.

"Please," I whisper, feeling another rush of heat between my thighs.

TJ kisses my shoulder. "No... Please what? What do you want, Millie?"

Silence stretches out between us as they wait for me to answer. But TJ never loosens his hold, and neither do Nate's eyes on mine.

What do I want? I want *them.* I want every bit of the pleasure they've promised.

I blow out a silent breath before I speak.

"I want you to make me come. Together. Now."

TJ sucks the side of my neck roughly before he growls. "We thought you'd never fucking ask."

I'm instantly lifted out of the pool, my bathing suit back in place, right into Nate's waiting arms. He sets me down, taking my hand as I hear water splashing, then see it pooled around TJ's feet before he flanks my other side.

Somehow, a towel is wrapped around my body as my feet scurry to keep up with them. I'm looking between them with a smile on my face because this is finally happening.

As we pass the attendant, who's come to meet us, she does a double take. "Sirs...ma'am?"

"We're leaving," Nate grinds out. "Make sure our girl gets her shit delivered to the room."

His crudeness makes me laugh. But he's a man on a mission. I press my lips together, glancing over at TJ, who just winks at me but holds my eyes.

"Should I cancel the rest of the services?" the woman calls out as we hurry away.

TJ ushers me through the double doors, never looking back as he shouts back.

"Ab-so-fucking-lutely."

sixteen

. . .

"When is it my turn? When do I get dicked down?"

millie

The ride up the elevator is torture. Pure fucking torture.

We're standing next to each other in this steel trap, surrounded by people because suddenly they're everywhere. Exactly when I don't want them to be.

Universe, you're drunk. Get off the sauce.

I swear just my proximity to them and their body heat is making my uterus twerk. But I have to stare straight ahead and try to pretend nobody's noticing that I'm in a towel, TJ's creating a small pool under his bare feet, and Nate is totally dry.

We're a spectacle. Especially since the guys look like serial killers doing nothing but staring at me like I'm dinner.

There's nothing to see here, folks. They're just gonna murder my vaginal walls. Please don't call the cops.

118

The elevator mercifully stops at our floor, and TJ takes my hand, almost knocking a man over as we exit. But I throw, "Sorry...so sorry," over my shoulder as I'm rushed out between them.

I haven't stopped giggling because I know I look like one of those professional marathon walkers. But my legs won't move any faster unless I start jogging.

A couple passes us, staring strangely. Deserved. But the boys are oblivious, even though I'm still laughing.

This is insane. Wild. And kind of a core memory.

"Need a key," Nate barks as we reach the door, turning back and motioning impatiently for it from TJ.

TJ frowns for a second before we all look at each other. *Oh...*

"Shit," he breathes out, finishing my thought as the collective realization hits us all at once.

In our fucking sex fog, it seems as if we left our stuff back in the locker rooms. I swear to god, the universe hates me. Why is this so difficult? All my friends get their fun.

Eleanor just showed up to her life and got railed by an NFL team. Her sister, Samantha, got snowed in by acci-dent...in California. It never snows there, and she got turned into an interoffice memo by her four bosses. They were hitting send all weekend.

When is it my turn? When do I get dicked down?

"Fuck. You've got to be kidding me," Nate grits out, taking my hand as TJ turns to look up and down the hallway.

The tension in Nate's jaw almost makes me frown until his eyes drop to mine. I swear for a split second it's as if he's considering sealing the deal out here in the open.

Well, shit. My lips press together.

"Bingo," TJ throws out, slapping Nate's shoulder.

My eyes bulge as I look down, unable to hide the humor on my face as I try not to give away that for a hot second, I thought TJ was answering Nate's thought.

TJ smirks, pointing. "Housekeeping. Be right back."

Nate and I watch him take off faster than light down the hallway. I start to turn toward Nate until I feel his hands on my shoulders, his rough fingers snaking down my spine.

"You're fucking gorgeous," he growls from behind me. "I swear to god, I'll bust this goddamn door down if he can't get us in."

I release a quiet whoosh, leaning into his touch. I feel like I might combust as I add, "Well, they already have to fix the air-conditioning on this side of the hotel. What's a door too?"

Nate's lips touch my neck, and I quietly moan before I shiver, still watching my sex lord and savior TJ be the hero we need.

He's speaking animatedly, making me bring the front of my towel up to my mouth to hide my smile as Nate keeps feathering kisses to my neck.

TJ points back to us, looking like he's begging her to let us in. And by the way her face is all scrunched up, she's not buying any of what he's saying. She may very well be the only woman his charm doesn't work on.

"That doesn't look promising," I whisper.

Nate hums into my skin, resting his hands on my hips. "If he can't get a key, I'll throw him through. Either way, Scrappy...you're gettin' fucked."

I suck in a breath, pressing my ass into him. I'm going to lose my mind.

Four things happen, all in order, to highlight the freaking calamity of this moment.

The housekeeper shakes her head no. TJ drops to his knees, begging again. I laugh. And Nate grumbly shouts, "Fuck it, I'll go."

He spins me around before looking me dead in the eye.

"Don't you fucking move from this spot. I will be right back."

I giggle, then nod. His lips press violently to mine, and I'm kissed...well, before he looks up, calling TJ, and stalks back toward the elevators.

My eyes drop to the spot where I'm standing, my fingers brushing over my lips as I whisper to myself, "Don't move from this spot. Got it, boss."

I smile again. Fucking giddy. My whole body, mind, and spirit feel like tipsy girl energy, definitely drunk on them.

As I look up across from me, the door opens, calling my eyes. One of the housekeeping staff walks out, smiling at me.

"Hi," I say cheerily, still in a goofy stupor.

I'm going to get very laid.

"Are you locked out?" she offers, motioning to the door.

I nod as my heart picks up its pace, and I'm answering like I've just discovered the answers to the cosmos. "Yes. I am."

My body's almost vibrating as the housekeeper reaches to her hip, taking a white key card in her hand, and closes the three steps to our door.

In what feels like slow motion, my head whips toward TJ, who's about ten feet away to my right, before switching to Nate, who's the same distance to my left.

All I know is thank god for birth control because I'd be willing to play Russian roulette with all things that can be cured with penicillin right now. Nothing is stopping me from getting tag-teamed multiple times after this edgefest.

She swipes her key. The beep sounds. And the door clicks.

TJ and Nate lock eyes on me, and I'm only half-sure I've said their names because it feels like the dinner bell just rang and we're starved.

"Thank you," I rush out as two giant men, one of them still wet, kick into gear and haul ass back toward the room.

I don't know if the lady even gets out of the way fast enough because the squeal that leaves my body is more than excited. I run inside into the tin can of a living room before I spin around, looking into their wild eyes.

Holy shit.

The second the door closes behind them, the energy suffocates us. Sex, desire, and lust fill the tiniest of cracks as we stand staring at each other in complete silence.

They look feral. And I'm wet.

I grate the bottom corner of my lip with my teeth, a grin on my face. My nipples are already showing up since it seems our air-conditioning has been fixed.

TJ swings his face to Nate's, smirking.

"Here's the play—first touch makes her come. Loser licks it off her thighs."

Oh. My. God. His gorgeous green eyes turn back to mine. "Ready. Set. Go."

Pandemonium breaks out.

The Tweedles shove each other playfully as I jump.

They're barreling toward me as I scream and laugh, only making it three steps through the bedroom door before TJ wraps an arm around my waist, scooping me up.

I'm folded over his veiny forearm, tucked into his side like a freaking football, and lifted off the ground before I land smack-dab on the bed with a bounce.

My laughter fills the room as I scramble to my knees, breathless, my eyes volleying between them, so turned on as they grin back.

There's no waiting or seduction.

We are getting down to business.

Nate's voice rumbles as he unties his trunks with one hand, looking at TJ. "Fuck her first. Worship her later?"

TJ nods, drawing out, "Yup," before shoving his wet trunks down and stepping out. I smile harder.

If this is how they get on the same page, I am forever in. My eyes drop to take TJ in, to see what I'm working with, before they dart back up to his. *Holy shit.*

His cock is settled against his toned stomach, heavy and in charge like it's leaning against a car saying, *Hey, Mama.*

TJ is huge. *There's no way that's fitting.*

"It'll fit, baby." He chuckles, reading my mind. "You just gotta take a couple deep breaths."

My hand covers my mouth, hiding my smile as I sit back on my haunches. I can't believe this is really happening. I'm about to fuck them porn-style.

I've never been more nervously excited for anything in my life.

Nate's deep baritone calls my attention, only to make

me bite my lip because his trunks are sliding over his delicious thighs now too.

"Clothes. Off. Now, Scrappy."

I swear I almost answer, *Yes, Sir.* Instead, I reach up behind my neck, keeping my eyes on TJ as I tug on the strings. They fall down over my collarbone before they take the yellow fabric triangles with them, freeing my breasts and eliciting growls from the boys.

I look at them from under my lashes before undoing the tie at my back and letting it completely fall off my body.

My nipples are pebbled, goose bumps spreading over my chest as they stare, taking me in, appreciating what they see.

I run a hand over my nipple, liking their eyes on me. I'd tell them to come and get me, but they're already stalking toward me, making my pulse shoot through the roof.

Good lord. They're going to fuck me into existentialism. I'll be questioning the meaning of life after this… because it may only be their cocks.

"Condoms are in the drawer," Nate grits out, coming at me from the bottom of the bed.

"Fuck that. I wanna feel her," TJ growls, coming at me from the side.

They're going to tear me apart.

"Birth control…" I squeal out, crawling backward while giggling. "I'm tested. Clean and on birth control. You?"

TJ's eyes hit the ceiling as he lets out a very appreciative *"Fuck yeah"* as Nate narrows his eyes on me.

"Looks like we get to fuck you raw, baby."

My ankle's grabbed as Nate drags me caveman-style

down the bed. TJ's hands are already pawing at my bikini bottoms.

I barely have time to register what's happening before I'm stripped of the last barrier I'm wearing, forcing me to roll sideways a little as I squeal.

Nate grabs my thigh, spreading my legs. "Ass to clit, baby."

His tongue hits directly where he promised as he starts at my ass, flipping me onto my back and licking me all the way fucking clean right through my fucking pussy.

"Fuck," I hiss.

My clit pulses, igniting a visceral reaction, and he slaps my thighs open wider as he seals over my clit.

He's a fucking animal. There's no gentleness. No easing me in. Nate wants, so he takes.

TJ chuckles. "Girlie, you're about to get rocked."

My eyes flutter, looking up at him. Definitely fucking rocked already.

Nate hums against my clit, and my stomach contracts. But TJ smirks. He comes closer to my face, and my lips part because I'm already panting.

I want his cock in my mouth.

I'm staring at it hungrily because it's thick and veiny, so fucking hard that it looks sculpted. I'm mesmerized, watching as he slowly trails his fingers up his shaft like he's teasing himself.

It makes me want to lick up to the rim before I run my tongue over the precum.

"Oh fuck," I breathe out as Nate's tongue does figure eights, making my hips rock and stealing my attention.

"Hey...me," TJ breathes out, calling me back with a wink.

Oh my god. This is the only way I want men fighting over me, forever.

He brings the strained head of his cock to my lips, teasing me as I open my mouth before he drags the glisten roughly over my bottom lip, smearing his arousal.

"Lick it off like my good little slut."

My breath catches in my throat. Our eyes connect as Nate thrusts his tongue inside my cunt and growls.

"*Fuck,*" I moan before I dart my tongue out, cleaning the saltiness from my lips. I whimper, my hips circling as I slide my hand to the top of Nate's head, fingers gripping his hair.

This is just as I'd imagined. Nate eats pussy like a pro. And TJ teases like one.

I'm breathing hard as Nate's tongue flattens over my clit, licking me clean before he sucks, drawing it between his lips, flicking his tongue over it quickly before letting it go.

"Oh my god," I let out. "That feels so good. Nate, don't stop. *Please.*"

My eyes close. The feeling of Nate between my thighs wrecks me, but TJ isn't done with me.

"Open," is growled from above me.

TJ's cock presses to my lips, so I lick them one more time before being *his* dirtiest slut, as requested.

He slides inside my warm mouth, taking his time. So I hollow my cheeks before I lift my other hand and caress his heavy sack.

His face snaps to mine. "Ooo, you wanna get fucked, Smalls? Keep going. See how I fill that pussy."

I hum around his cock, feeling Nate spread me open. My lust coating my pussy as he cleans, nipping at my clit.

I swear my legs are already shaking as TJ feeds me more of his cock.

"Suck it, baby. Show me that throat."

The back of my throat is tickled by TJ's cock just as Nate pulls away and spits on my cunt. "I'm gonna eat you every fucking day."

The breath I draw in makes me suck TJ harder. His head falls back, eyes on the ceiling, before he starts controlling the moment.

TJ grips his cock, his eyes holding mine as he feeds me just enough before depriving me again.

My hips are rolling now. Undulating. Begging. I'm so close because I've basically been here all day. Wanting and needing them. Fucking desperate to come.

I grip Nate's hair tighter, earning a growl from him, and his palm flattens on my stomach, holding me still.

He's fucking relentless, licking and sucking, working my clit over and over, humming into it.

I want to tell him not to stop. That I'm so close. But TJ's cock cuts off all my sound, and his voice activates another rush of slickness. "Don't you fucking make her come. Her pussy's mine, you dick."

Nate lets go of my clit with a pop just as TJ thrusts into my mouth, hitting my throat.

"Tell her that," Nate chuckles as I keep trying to pull his head back between my thighs.

"Bad girls get punished, Millie," TJ growls, thrusting inside again and grabbing my throat. "Swallow my fucking cock this time."

I do, losing all my air, staring into TJ's eyes as tears trickle from the sides.

"Atta girl. Take it all."

His thumb rubs over my skin, and I know he wants to feel himself.

TJ and I are suspended, staring at each other as Nate eats me, adding two thick fingers. He thrusts them inside my pussy, curling them to hit the exact spot to make my legs weak.

The need for air begins to burn. TJ pulls out as I gasp, and a thread of spit stays connected between the head of TJ's cock and my bottom lip.

"Fuck me," I breathe out heavily, not caring who does it, just needing it done. Now.

I don't have to ask twice because my body is left cold, all hands off, making my stomach contract and my throat gasp over the loss. Nate's eyes are hooded and demanding as he breathlessly wipes the back of his hand over his mouth and rolls me on my side, throwing my leg over TJ's waist.

TJ darts his hand between us, sliding his middle finger inside my pussy before drawing out my lust all over his finger.

I blink, thrown off-kilter, but he smirks, only offering, "Jealous," before he licks me off his fucking finger. My heart stops. *Jealous?* He wants what Nate had.

Nate closes in behind me, making me shift my head over my shoulder. But it's TJ who speaks.

"Damn, she tastes like good pussy. Real...good... pussy." His voice lowers. "Wanna try?"

Something about how he says it draws my eyes back to his just as he smiles and kisses me. Our tongues mingle, but we're sloppy, lips gliding over one another's with the kind of desperation that only comes from lust.

Pure fucking lust.

Suddenly, the room feels humid, as if our body heat is

pouring out, trying to set us on fire. It feels electric, like my chemical makeup has finally been brought to life.

Hands are all over me. And mine are on them, ghosting over flesh, rubbing and kneading. They're cupping my breasts and pinching my nipples, each of them always somewhere the other isn't.

Nate spreads my ass cheeks as TJ kisses my pussy into every corner of my mouth. I'm overwhelmed in the best sense. I don't know whose hands are whose, and I don't care.

All my thoughts have been hijacked, and all that's left is them.

Nate's finger rubs, pressing to my puckered hole before lube hits my ass. It makes my shoulders jump and a giggle melt into our bubble.

"Stay still," Nate growls, making me laugh again.

TJ's hand cradles my face as Nate trails kisses up my back, branding me with his words.

"I want to fuck you here." His fingertip slips inside my ass, but he keeps it there, teasing me. "I wanna fill your ass with my cock while you let TJ fuck your cunt." His chest presses to my back. "Is that what you want, Millie? For us to defile this body and ruin you for everyone else?"

I'm nodding my head, humming. But Nate already knows the fucking answer. I keep my mouth attached to TJ's, pressing back into Nate, shamelessly rubbing my ass against him and his finger.

He pulls it out, gripping my hip with his other hand just below where TJ's is. We're writhing, breaths picking up, chests rising and falling faster and faster as Nate and TJ grind into me.

Nate runs his hand from my hip to my face guiding it

over my shoulder, raising up so he can kiss me too. It's hard and claiming, his fingers gripping my jaw.

God, he's so fucking dominant.

I rub my clit up and down TJ's cock as Nate owns my mouth aggressively, our bodies getting sweatier before TJ reaches down, angling his cock.

"You might wanna take that deep breath now, baby."

Nate holds my jaw, not letting me go as TJ runs his fingers under my hair, gripping it at the nape of my neck before he sinks inside my pussy.

Nate's tongue dives inside my mouth, eating the drawn-out *"Fuck"* I release in unison with TJ.

TJ's cock stretches me instantly, and it stings but in the way that makes you want the pain. To crave it. There's no way. I can hear myself breathing, feel the explosion of goose bumps prickling my skin as my lips part.

"You're so big," I say breathlessly. "I—"

My body quivers, cutting off my words as my nipples grow harder because TJ's grip tightens in my hair, holding me still.

"Shh, shh. You can take it. Look at me, baby." I do instantly, lashes fluttering as he pushes deeper, shuddering at the feeling. His restrained words are guttural. "Open that pussy for me. Take this cock. All of it."

Nate's hand shoves my leg higher, opening me wider for TJ to push inside my slick walls further, making me moan loudly.

"Fuck. TJ. It feels so good."

"Good girl," Nate growls from behind. "You look so beautiful taking his cock. Your pussy wants it bad. So let him feed it."

I'm already panting, rocking my hips forward for

more as Nate whispers in my ear, kissing the lobe, "Relax for me, Mills."

I feel his cock rimming my ass, so I stop rocking, and TJ kisses me again. His cock jumps inside me, and it makes me clench around him.

"Fuck you," TJ hums into my mouth. "You're definitely getting punished."

One of Nate's hands spreads my ass before he begins pressing inside, not even getting the tip in. The sound leaving my lungs is guttural and choked.

"Oh...my god. Nate. Fuck."

More lube drizzles over my hole, and I hear the crude sounds of him spreading it quickly over his cock, stroking himself behind me. He kisses my neck, then my shoulder, as TJ caresses my breast.

Nate's voice makes my eyes close. "Baby, your ass is so tight. I wanna be rough. Tell me I can be."

TJ bites my bottom lip, rolling his hips and pumping inside me a few times. "Let us use you. We'll make it hurt so good."

I lick my lips, reaching back to grab Nate's ass and squeezing my pussy around TJ's cock again, feeling really good at being bad.

"Fuck me how you want. Just don't fall in love with me. We expire on Sunday."

"Deal," they say in unison before TJ's jaw tenses.

Nate's hand bears down on my shoulder as he grits out, "Hold her," just as I feel the head of his cock pass my rigid barrier.

I moan, squeezing my eyes shut, my hip held still by TJ. Fuck, this feeling is mind-blowing. We're unmoving and breathless, each of us almost shivering from being so connected.

It's pain and pleasure married in delicious depravity. And it's coursing through me...through *us*. Nate drags out again, TJ's eyes checking in on me, but I bite my lip, wanting his again.

"Jesus, you're fucking perfect," Nate exhales, frozen in place.

"So perfect," TJ whispers against my lips, his eyes closed.

Their cocks fight for space inside me, making me fuller than I've ever been. And it's the kind of bliss I hope to know again and again.

TJ moves first, rolling his hips, filth falling from his lips.

"You feel that, baby?" he growls deeply, bottoming out and stealing my breath. "Fuck...your body's a greedy little bitch. You swallowed both of us. Now, let's see if I can make that cunt cry before Nate comes in that sweet little ass."

Before I can say anything, Nate begins fucking me too, dragging his cock in and out, stretching the ring, soothing the burn with each thrust.

I feel removed from my body, encompassed by this feeling, the friction between our bodies moving in unison.

We're already chasing our release.

Our legs are a tangle as we rock together. Sweat gathers between us, their hands staying on me and mine on them.

Compelled to hold on to this connection.

"Make me come," I breathe, whimpering, digging my nails into TJ's back.

He's holding my hair with one hand, the other gripped on my thigh as he fucks me faster. His breath is heavy, shared between our kiss as his tongue dives inside my mouth. But when he pulls away, he grunts, powering into me, bouncing my body.

"Yes, yes, yes...I need to—"

"Beg me," TJ cuts in. "Beg me to fucking come."

Nate thrusts behind me, his giant hands anchored to my shoulder as he picks up speed fucking me raw. "Not yet, Millie. You come with me."

Oh my god. My body trembles as they relentlessly fuck me, their cocks rubbing the thin walls that separate them. Over and over. Making my mind splinter. Everything is too much and not enough.

God, this feels too good. Too fucking good.

"Please...I want to come," I groan, trying to move my leg so I can rub my clit against TJ's stomach like a fucking brat. But he holds me in place, hammering into my pussy, his eyes narrowed in on me as that muscle ticks in his jaw.

"Don't you fucking move, Millie. I said beg. Do you hear me? Are you my slut? Cuz I make them come."

"Or mine..." Nate growls behind me. "I said you come with me. Keep your mouth shut."

I can't speak. Even if I keep trying, words won't come out because they've sent me spinning.

Nate's cock meets TJ's rhythm, and it's infuriating. Because I'm possessed by it, teased, edged, and fucking needy.

TJ won't let me have what I want. And Nate's demanding I obey.

My words finally find their freedom, ringing out.

"Nate... Ahh, goddammit." My voice is pleading, even though I don't want it to be. "TJ... Fuck you two. I wanna come. I wanna come."

TJ sucks hard on my neck, marking me. "You made us wait for this pussy. Now you'll wait too."

I scratch at TJ's back, slapping Nate's thigh, whining, mewling, growling like a goddamn animal.

"I'm close," Nate growls into my back, adding, "Let her come."

"Please." My voice spills out, barely a whisper, my eyes locked on TJ's before I repeat myself. "Please make me come all over your cock."

TJ jerks my body flush before they both piston inside me, and my clit finally feels the friction it needed.

"Yes," I cry out, reaching for them.

The build hits me so hard that I'm instantly climbing and climbing, moaning into TJ's tensed jaw as Nate's teeth scrape my shoulder. I swear he wants to bite me like lions do their fucking mates.

But we're animals. Hedonism central. Fucking faster and faster. Harder and harder. As they hammer inside me, making the smell of sex fill the air, my hips rock quickly, not a single part of their body untouching mine.

"You're so beautiful" is whispered into my back as "Yes. Fuck me so good, baby" comes from the front.

Their foreheads rest against my head as we rock together, fucking each other empty. I swallow, my mouth hanging open as I grind closer to TJ.

I'm panting, my entire body tensing up, stomach contracting.

"Oh god, oh god, oh god," I chant.

"Good girl. Come with me," Nate growls, slapping my ass and making me cry out. "Let me ruin this ass, baby."

I'm at the edge of my orgasm, my body begging to fall. My hand dives between my legs, giving myself even more friction, and I stick my fingers between TJ's stomach and my clit.

That's all I need.

The hushed scream rises in my throat, unable to break free because my body is assaulted by the explosion that's been waiting.

I come. So. Fucking. Hard.

My body is jostled as TJ and Nate don't hold back. I'm fucked stupid as I keep coming, the deep groan that was trapped finally bursting out.

Nate's still gripping my ass, smacking it again before he groans my name, spreading my ass cheeks as he comes, his entire body engulfing me from behind.

TJ's mouth seals over mine, swallowing my cries as he grunts, drilling inside me over and over as he grits out his words, lost to the feeling.

"I'm gonna... get...you fucking pregnant."

He jerks two more times before stilling inside me, filling me with his cum.

I can't move, let alone speak, as my heart beats out of my chest.

"Millie, fuck..." Nate breathes, pulling out to let some of his cum coat my asshole and drip down to my leg as he breathes hard.

TJ's nuzzling my neck, pressing kisses to my skin as I feel him shake with a quiet laugh. Just like me. Because that was fucking wild.

Nate smirks, kissing my cheek before running his fingers up and down my back. We're sated and blissful, nobody needing to fill the silence as we lie there in our beautiful filth.

Seconds turn to minutes as we cuddle in the nude, TJ

still inside me before his softened cock finally abandons me, making me shiver.

Nate's fingers gather what's left of himself on my leg before he drags it over and pushes it inside my cunt, making me suck in a breath.

"Jealous," he whispers, swiping it inside me once more.

I lie there, spent and out of breath, but I chuckle. "For two people excellent at sharing, you're not good at sharing."

Nate growls, wrapping an arm around my waist and pulling me closer to him, making TJ frown.

I grin but roll over, my lips instantly accepted by my favorite defensive end.

Nate kisses me slowly and deliberately as we cuddle, TJ scooting in behind me. His body melds to mine, and still, none of us speaks.

Seven days…that's all we have for this little slice of heaven.

I take a deep breath, a full smile blooming.

"Sooo, how long do you two take to recover because I'm still waiting for the part where one of you makes me come and the other licks it off."

Deep chuckles are all I hear before they attack, tickling me senseless. Nate throws me over his shoulder as TJ follows, and we all walk into the bathroom.

Guess round two's in the shower.

Alexa, play "Perfect Day" from Legally Blonde.

seventeen

. . .

"Round two or revenge? Whaddya think?"

millie

I wake up like someone's given me a shot of adrenaline straight to the heart. Because we're late. We have mischief to get to, and we overslept. *Dammit.*

My head shifts around as I sit up in a tangle of muscular legs and sexy fucking backs.

"Shit," I rush out, slapping the two bare assess on each side of me. "Wake up."

Damn, those butts are nice.

Last night was one for the books. We went three rounds in total. And I was half-convinced I would wake up in a coma. But thankfully, I'm just in need of some ibuprofen.

Plus, there's revenge ahead, and that means there's no rest for the wicked.

Grumbles and groans come from under pillows and a

137

blanket, so I slap their asses again. Multiple times. *Because why not?*

"Boys. Get up. We're gonna be late for surfing. Don't you want to see our handiwork live and in person? I'm positive the rash hasn't gone away."

"I bet he looks like that shit my oldest sister's kids get…hand, foot, and mouth, but all over," TJ jokes before yawning and rolling over, fully erect.

Oh my. It never gets old to see it saluting me.

He's grinning as he takes that big-ass dick in his hand, but I shake my head.

"We don't have time for that."

Nate grabs me around the waist, pulling me in and pressing his face to my lady luck, but I push him away, laughing.

"We're going to be late. Get up."

Neither moves. In fact, they lie there, nude, on their backs, stroking themselves.

I let out a heavy breath, but TJ pushes his bottom lip out as Nate speaks.

"Scrappy…we just wanna cuddle." He shrugs, and I narrow my eyes, giving in to laughter as he finishes the thought. "Naked. With our cocks inside you."

I don't care how cute and pouty they are. I wave my hand in finality.

"No… Absolutely. Not."

"Fuck." I breathe harder as Nate grips my hips from behind.

"Look at him, baby," he grits out. "You fucking look at

him while you come all over my cock."

I'm staring up at TJ through my lashes, body jostled over and over as Nate pounds me from behind. TJ's hand tightens in my hair, and he rolls his hips as I suck and swallow, my fingers gripping the sheets for support.

I am being thoroughly fucked on all fours. The two of them hammer in a punishing rhythm, harder and harder, destroying my body.

And I love every fucking minute.

My pussy was already sore from last night, but it didn't seem to matter because I was so wet Nate slipped right in. Not that it would've mattered. After last night, I've learned I like a little pain with my pleasure. Just the thought makes me moan.

"Do it again," TJ growls, so I obey...drawing the sound out, watching his head fall back as he draws out of my mouth and pushes back in.

Nate groans, tightening his grip on my hips.

"Fuck. What are you thinking about, baby?" I start to answer but he changes direction speaking to TJ, "She just strangled my dick. Let her speak."

TJ's cock drags out from between my lips sloppily. He stares down, drunk with lust as he fists his cock, jerking himself off in front of my face.

"Answer him."

That's all he says, and it's hot.

"I was thinking about getting spanked again," I say, breathless.

TJ smirks and slaps his dick against my cheek before rubbing the head over my lips and shoving back inside my hollowed cheeks. "Mmmm, suck it, baby. Swallow Daddy's cock."

My body shudders, only electrified by the feel of Nate's hand on my ass.

Oh god. Yes.

Nate's body slaps against my skin, his cock bottoming out with each thrust. He fucks my cunt mercilessly before I feel the first delicious sting ignite my ass.

A strangled scream releases around TJ's dick, followed by another smack.

"That's it. Squeeze that cunt," Nate growls. "There's my good girl."

TJ's groaning and grunting, his words unintelligible as he takes over fucking my face. His hands come to the side of my head, holding me in place as he hits the back of my throat.

I gag, but he keeps going.

"Come on, baby, swallow it back. Let me come down that fucking throat."

I'm bobbing my head faster and faster, my pussy filled from behind, feeling like I'm going to explode. I want to come. To scream around TJ's cock while Nate comes inside me.

I'm completely in their control, fucked from each end.

Gagging. Spit gathering around my lips. Pussy clenched, contracting, begging.

I feel Nate's other hand reach around and rub my needy clit, and I almost collapse. My knees spread wider on the bed, but Nate wraps an arm around me, his body hunched over mine as he holds me up.

"Come with us. Millie, fucking come with us."

TJ's fucking my mouth, his chest heaving, breath stuttered. And I know he's there. I can feel his balls draw up.

I'm soaked in my lust and theirs as we fuck. Harder

and harder. Gripping and grabbing each other. Running down our fucking release like wild animals.

"My dirty fucking whore. This is what you get...you get fucked. Suck that dick."

Oh god. Yes.

"That's it. Let me fill that cunt with my cum. I'm gonna watch it drip out down your thighs, and you're not washing it off. I own this cunt."

Mewling is my only answer. But that's cut off by TJ's cock.

I can't breathe, eyes watering until he pulls out, jacking himself again as I suck in a breath.

"Make me come, you fucking slut."

His cock slips back between my used lips, and I suck, hollowing out my cheeks, knowing he's about to spurt cum down my throat.

My clit is so swollen it hurts, but Nate rubs circles, hitting my G-spot with each thrust. He's rolling his cock into my pussy, grinding into me, so I push my ass back to meet every movement.

Tension builds, higher and higher. I can feel it in my stomach, through my body, making me writhe in Nate's arms.

"Take it, Millie. Take what you need."

I'm grinding into his fingers, pussy fucked, mouth full, as white light begins to pepper my vision. And then I'm gone. Cresting.

Coming so fucking hard that I don't feel how hard TJ pulls my hair fucking my mouth before his stomach tenses and his cum fills my throat. And I don't feel the bruises that will most definitely be left on my body by Nate's grip on my waist as he fucks me intensely until my pussy is filled.

All I feel is bliss.

TJ's cock drags from my lips as my arms give out. Nate lets me lie face down on the bed, kissing my spine over and over.

"Hey," I hear from above, so I try and shift my head to look at TJ, but I can't.

He squats down, kissing the tip of my nose and looking me in the eye.

"Round two or revenge? Whaddya think?"

I laugh. I hate them.

But they're definitely good times. I think I'm starting to like this ho-mance.

eighteen

. . .

"His Timothée Chalamet arms must be burning."

tweedles

nate

TJ chuckles again, getting a *look* from Millie as the surf instructor makes his third comment about punctuality.

We *may* have been late. But it's only because Millie gave in to round two. So, she shouldn't be giving us looks since it was all about making *her* come again.

She leans over, her bikini-clad body touching my arm, making it flex as she not at all inconspicuously cups a hand to my ear and starts whispering like we're in high school.

"He keeps giving me rashy-faced looks. Should I ignore it or act like I hate him?" *Act like?*

Who, I mouth, full of bullshit, not interested in *Chad* as

I stare forward like I'm listening to how to mount the board.

Even though when we arrived, seeing him in a head-to-toe scuba suit made TJ lose his shit. He couldn't stop laughing because the dude looks like a horror flick. She fucked him up with that seaweed. And now he's covered except for his blotchy face that's pinched in the face cutout.

But what stood out to me is that Chad didn't seem to have learned his lesson back at the club. Because the way he kept trying to get closer to her to say something made me want to toss him like in the Olympics when those dudes spin in a circle.

I turn to Millie because she hasn't said anything; she's just staring at my profile. I raise my brows, but she nudges me, making me grin.

Millie glances at Chad, then back to me in answer to my question, but I grimace and reach out to lift her onto my lap.

Damn, her smile's beautiful.

"I didn't know it was an act," I finally answer quietly to her face, but she rolls her eyes, shushing me before keeping her voice low.

"You know what I mean. Engage or don't engage? You're the guru."

"Pay attention to me," I growl back, nuzzling her neck as she laughs and wraps her arms around me in a hug, scratching my back gently.

Aww fuck, she turns me into mush. From Rottweiler to Golden Retriever. I could stay like this for hours.

The instructor drones on, so I lean back after she releases me, digging my hands into the sand. Her legs are stretched out to the side of me, a few strands of her hair blowing in the breeze, and it's fucking something.

Something that has my dick jumping.

I know she feels it because her shoulders shake until her attention is stolen. TJ's smiling, staring at her before he lays his head on her lap.

Her fingers brush through his hair like it's the most natural thing in the world to be sitting on my lap with his head on hers.

My brows draw together, a thought brewing until the instructor claps.

"All right, everyone. Girls are with Scottie, and dudes with me."

TJ's up, freeing her before she turns back to me, her finger gently poking my chest.

"Listen, no shhmurder...but...if Chad gets eaten by a shark, that's the lord's will." She points between me and Teej. "You two stay on the board."

I laugh as Eleanor reaches for Millie's hands and helps her up. They're laughing, hooking arms as they walk away, their feet swishing in the sand and kicking it up.

TJ looks back at me, raising his brows before both our eyes land on her again.

"You think she'll be mad that we bodyguarded her?" he laughs as we stand up.

I chuckle, answering honestly, "Who cares? Fuck Chad."

Crew strolls up with his arms crossed, looking between us. It's nice to finally see him, considering he and Eleanor haven't been out of the room.

"Damn...looks like I missed some shit." He cocks his head as TJ and I look at each other. "You two like the girl." He's supposed to think that, but why does it feel like we've been caught? His eyes narrow on us. "That's a first, huh? I thought this was just a vacation thing. More importantly, what does Mills think?"

I clear my throat, not wanting any fucking part of this conversation. And I can tell TJ feels the same. But we're here to sell it, so I shrug.

"Nah, she's cool. We're not labeling shit. It's all good. You know we'd never do her dirty, man."

Crew frowns, the same way he does when we miss a play on the field. Millie's his girl's bestie, and that makes her unfuck-aroundable-with. And he's about to say as much, but TJ interjects.

Smoke and mirrors, baby.

"You know, Crew...maybe, and I mean maybe—" He holds up his hands, bullshit written all over his face. "— we were actually just staring at your future wife."

That'll do it. There's nothing he hates more than when we bring up his honeymoon. Crew's brows hit his fucking hairline. And I'm pretty sure he might take a *"just joking, not joking"* swing at TJ.

TJ chuckles, taking a step backward and getting ready to run as he adds, "Because we did fu—"

He doesn't get the rest out as Crew lunges for him, chasing him down toward the water, and I yell, "Don't break his arms, Crew. We need him next season."

I grab my board, my eyes landing on Millie once again before I head down, ready to drown Chad any chance I get. And try to figure out why that moment with her in my lap and TJ in hers won't leave my mind.

tj

Nate and I can't even look at each other. We can't. Because fucking *Chad*. I blow out a shaky breath, trying to keep a straight face—unsuccessfully, as Crew chuckles too.

We paddled out ten minutes ago, but Chad's been having some trouble.

The kind me and Nate caused. And now can't stop fucking laughing over.

"Dude, are you good?" Crew throws out, unimpressed with this asshole.

I literally suck my whole bottom lip behind my top teeth to not laugh.

"I'm fine. The board's just slippery," Chad snaps before looking at the instructor. "Did you even wax this?"

Surf dude nods, watching with a grin, like us, as Chad slaps a hand on his board, trying to hold himself still again. It's like watching a car wreck. I can't look away.

The board wobbles as he tries to sit, and my brows shoot up, waiting for it. He's shaking like a leaf on a tree, making his blotchy cheeks flutter and his ass slide.

Oh fuck. I have to stare down at the water because I've never needed to laugh so fucking hard in my life. And to make it worse, involuntary laughter keeps coming out of Nate's stupid-ass mouth.

I shake my head, snapping my fingers at him, still not looking his way as I speak. "Keep it together...fucking keep it together."

My voice is so strained, way too much laughter about to burst.

But if I do, then the fucking surf instructor and Crew

might figure out that two vigilantes may have mixed coconut oil with Chad's wax when he wasn't looking.

Because it's good for assholes and reefs, apparently.

The great thing about mixing it is that it's not really an obvious problem until water hits.

I learned that one from my youngest sister, who got sick and tired of her boyfriend never asking if she wanted something to drink when he was getting his own. She told me, "If we ain't drinking, he ain't drinking."

She poured everything from the fridge into glass jars and then mixed his hand lotion with oil. Condensation's a bitch.

Bro had a lot of glass to clean up.

Crew shakes his head, lying down and paddling, only saying, "I'm going out. Have fun with that," before he shows off for Eleanor.

I give a salute as Nate fucking giggles again like a little girl in pigtails, his shoulders rising as he looks over to where Millie is, still trying to stop laughing. *Goddammit, he's the worst.*

As long as we don't look at each other, we can get away with this.

Jesus, I spoke too soon. "*Ehhaheeehahha,*" comes out of Chad's mouth as he wobbles again, looking like a seal on a teeter-totter.

"You doing okay there, buddy? Try using your core."

Nate squeezes his eyes closed with a fist covering his mouth. But I throw more gasoline on the fire.

"You almost got it, champ."

My jaw tenses as laughter tries to spill out. But Nate slaps his board, shouting his words, trying to cover up our nonsense.

"Let's fucking goooo! Surfing is awesome."

What the fuck is he saying? I'm crumbling. Bits of what I'm holding in start to bubble out. I splash some water on my face to hide the fact that I'm literally starting to cry. I eke out my words in way too high-pitched a voice. "Let's do this. I'm ready to grind."

I have to turn my head as Chad tips forward and back this time, knocking his forehead on the board.

"I've got this," Chad rages, even though nobody asked.

"Hell yeah," our instructor cheers, picking up the completely wrong vibe. But seeing as he's looking at us with the most bloodshot eyes, I'm thinking he's not catching on anytime soon. "Dudes, we can just rip all day if you guys want. That's the coolest part of these private sessions. No people equals no traffic."

I clear my voice a few times, hard, holding back before losing it completely.

It's the fact that Chad's all mad, with his little face poking out from the fucking scuba suit, all pissed off and even redder than before.

He's just trying so hard.

Holding the sides of the board, his hands keep slipping. And every time he stutters the beginnings but no ends of words in time with the wiggle.

His Timothée Chalamet arms must be burning.

Nate and I are watching, mesmerized, and the minute he actually starts to balance, Nate begins cheering, "Oh...oh...oh..."

But back in the water Chad goes.

I look up at the sky, catching Nate wiping an eye before I punch my thigh, trying to play it cool but knowing I'm not.

"Hey," Chad barks to the surf dude. "There's something wrong with this board. And I would know because I surfed with Kelly Slater."

"Not Kelly Slater," Nate barely gets out, making me cover my eyes with the butt of my hands.

But Chad ignores us and keeps yapping.

"You need to take this board back and bring me one that works."

Hightide draws his head back like he's lagging before he says, "Whoa...your energy is a lot, dude. Maybe what you need is the big foam boards we give kids?"

That's it. We're cooked.

We fucking lose it. We can't even be discreet.

Nate howls, and I unleash. We're laughing so hard no sound is coming out. Just a continuous wheeze, like a balloon slowly losing air. I lie back on my board, holding my side. "Fuck, my stomach hurts. Stop. I can't take it."

Chad doesn't think we're as funny.

"Oh, hilarious," Chad snaps at us like a little Chihuahua. "I could break an arm on an unproperly waxed board. Do you know how much my hands are insured for?" I take a breath, calming down as he keeps going. "Why don't you ask your girlfriend. Or maybe she's doesn't care about my *milly* since she's trying so hard to be yours."

The fuck?

"Not trying," I say, taking a breath. "Is."

He claps back. "Until you're done with her, right? Because that's what cleat chasers are for."

All the laughter stops. Full fucking stops.

I sit up, humor drained from my body.

"What the fuck did you just say?" Nate shouts.

I wipe a wet hand down my jaw. "What pisses you off

more, Chad...that you fumbled the ball or that we scored with an interception?"

Chad shrugs, bold as fuck trying to act like he doesn't care. But it's fucking clear we've gotten right under his boiled, rashy skin.

"You can have her."

What he says hangs there for a minute. And I know Nate's thinking the same fucking thing I am: *This mother-fucker ain't making it back to shore.*

I start to move off my board. I'm not sure what I'm going to do, but I know it's probably illegal.

Chad holds up a hand like he wants to reason with us.

"You don't have to be intimidated. I know she's probably talked about me. Maybe even still does. But I'm not competitive like that, man. There's always room at my table. Plus, we should be friends, dudes...I was literally there first. So I can help you get out when it's time. Cuz you know she's a clinger."

I hear Nate growl to himself, and I feel myself nodding, but it's not in agreement with Chad. It's with the kind of quiet violence men like us are good for on the field. We're gonna fuck him up.

Run right through him.

He better have State Farm on speed dial. He's going to need to cash in.

"She's clingy?" I level, watching him swallow. *Be nervous, you little prick.* "Why? Because she was gonna tell you she loved you?"

"You're a dick," Nate grits out next to me. "And we're gonna make you wish you hadn't said that."

All Chad's smugness is gone, replaced with fear. Fuck breaking his arm. I'm going to put him in a full-body cast over what he just said about her. But first...

151

"You don't fucking look at her," I level.

Nate points at him. "And you don't fucking speak to her."

I clasp my hands together hard. "She's a goddamn stranger to you."

Surf dude holds up his hands, looking between us.

"Whoa. Dudes. We've got a lot of energy happening. We just need to chill. Accidents on the water aren't good. Let's take it to shore."

Chad's already swimming away, pushing his board to bodysurf in since he can't get his slimy ass on it. But Nate and I keep staring at him.

The instructor follows, but we still sit and watch. Something in my peripheral catches my attention, making me look.

Dolphins. I'll be damned. There looks to be three or four, and they're all heading toward Chad.

I tap Nate's shoulder with the back of my hand, pointing, knowing he'll know exactly what I'm thinking.

He smirks. "I feel like we should show what we got, Teej. Catch some waves. Maybe help Chad get to the shore quicker."

"Absolutely. It's the right thing, seeing as he wants to be friends. And there's nothing like a crime of opportunity."

We paddle, arms digging into the water before catching the break and standing. We're no Kelly Slater, but we definitely know what we're doing.

Nate cuts in by Chad first, going right over his board, making him shout and the damn thing break. *We'll fucking pay for it.*

Chad's momentum is lost, and now he's just floating.

So it's my turn. I do the same, blindsiding him,

causing him to get half drowned by a wave. We're not going to hurt him, but we are going to scare the shit out of him.

So, before I'm too far, I cup my hands over my mouth and bellow, "Shark," pointing at the dolphins.

Funny thing about fins, it's hard to tell when you're in the water which ones want to eat you and which ones are from a Disney movie.

"Help," explodes into the sky behind me as Nate and I ride the rest of the way in with smiles on our faces.

Fuck you, Chad.

nineteen

· · ·

"Oh my god. What's that smell?"

millie

"That was harder than I thought it would be," Elle throws out, lying on the surfboard as she suns herself on the beach.

I laugh. "Well, technically, we never got up, so I don't think we even did the hard part. So far, we're just the trailer for *Blue Crush*."

"Oh my god, I love that movie. So underrated."

I nod, stretching as I watch the boys out on the water. They look like they're laughing.

"Right," I add, finally tearing my eyes away. "Wait, didn't the main character meet a pro quarterback in that movie?"

Eleanor laughs. "Guess I'm living the dream. Speaking of, where is Crew?"

"Rinsing off in those little hut showers over there. Do you even listen when he speaks?"

"Only when he's saying how great I am."

I grin, my eyes finding the guys again. A laugh bubbles out as I watch them in the distance because it looks like they're laughing too.

What is so funny? But then I see Chad next to them. *Nope, now he's in the water.* God, and the salt water must be stinging his face so bad.

Good.

Eleanor lowers her glasses, giving me that look. The one where she's formulating an opinion.

"It's nice to see you smile. I assume the Tweedles are to blame for that?"

I give a shoulder pop, unwilling to deny or confirm. But she narrows her eyes on me before looking to the tanned instructor, who's been sitting at the bottom of my board this whole time.

She mouths, *What the fuck?* to me, and I nod because clearly, he's a narc.

"Hey, wave runner. If you're going to sit there, you might as well turn around and hang out," she calls to him, but he shakes his head.

"They were very clear," he shouts loud enough to carry back. "The big one with the tattoos said, 'Watch the girl, but keep your eyes to yourself.' And then his friend told me that if she gets hurt—" He's pointing over his shoulder at me. I'm *she.* "—that he'd turn me into a live-action SpongeBob. Then he recited the first verse."

I laugh again, shaking my head as Elle rolls her eyes. "I'll give you a hundred bucks if you AirPod it so we can talk shit."

My eyes pop open, a little embarrassed and equally impressed she gamed the system so quickly. But he gives a thumbs-up, pulling some from his pocket before her head shifts in my direction.

"You like them, Mills—"

I shake my head. "We're cool. It's just some fun."

Her brows rise. "And I'm pretty sure they like you. Because we're on a private beach, and they put a bodyguard on you. Who's getting to you? Nemo?"

I narrow my eyes but scrunch my nose and grin. "I'm pretty sure we both know who they're keeping away. Because he who shall not be named made a big deal of trying to talk to me. At the club and in the elevator...today."

She lowers her glasses back over her judgy eyes. "Mmhm. Just remember, they never date the girls they fuck."

"I know, Mom—that's why we're fucking. Makes it so we don't date." I sigh before taking a sip of my water. "You were the one pushing me into this."

She starts to counter just as I think, *Why am I really fighting over a fake relationship?* However, that's not what cuts her off.

Moonbeam saunters up, wringing out her purple hair, all her bangles shimmering in the sun.

"You're missing out on a spiritual experience, ladies," she shames playfully like we're best friends.

Damn. I *should* hate her. She's my ex's new girlfriend. The new me.

But honestly, she's not that bad. And I dig her style.

The minute she spotted me, TJ, and Nate on the beach, she wrapped me in a whole-body hug that felt...overtly sexual but also genuine. Then, she took off the red amethyst hanging low around her neck and put it on mine, saying, "For stamina," with a wink.

How can you hate someone like that?

Eleanor breaks the memory, her voice dipped in audacious sincerity.

"How are you with *Chad*?"

"Elle," I throw out, chuckling, trying to shut her down, but she doesn't care.

Eleanor props herself up this time. "Is he holding you hostage? Are you running from the law? I don't get it. Because my bomb little queen over here has always been too good for him. And you're breathing, so you are too."

Moonbeam smiles, her eyes tracking Scottie, the instructor. I glance at him, eyes widening over the way he's looking at her.

Oh shit. Looks like their private time might lead to time with each other's privates.

The universe just keeps giving me presents.

She plays with the shells she has tied in her hair, eye-fucking Scottie before she answers. "The all-seeing goddess knows what we need. She always puts me in the right places. I just have to be open to accepting her gifts." Her eyes land on me now. "Never doubt that. And you'll have the time of your life."

Oh, moon's found the sun?

I'm celebrating in my head before I realize she's doing that eye contact thing again. So I lie back on my beached board, closing the windows to my soul.

Eleanor whispers my name, drawing my face to hers as Moonbeam closes in on Scottie.

"What are the chances she hasn't come once with *Chad* since she's been here. And that's why she passed on the stamina crystal."

I'm laughing silently as Eleanor sticks out her tongue at me. Before we grow quiet, just listening…as in eavesdropping on Moonbeam and Scottie's conversation.

"Have you ever seen sharks out here?"

"Not really out here," he draws out. "They have this intense energy. I locked eyes with one once, and it changed me. Spiritually. Just opened my mind to endless possibilities."

"That's like divination," she exhales, and I imagine her lifting her hands and waving them over him as she speaks. "Your aura is so open. So free. And very sexual. There are a lot of colors. I see red, orange, yellow...I even see indigo and violet."

Eleanor's voice never misses a beat on the other side of me. "That would be a rainbow...either she thinks he's a leprechaun, or Beam's asking just how open surf boy is?"

Oh my god. But my laughter cuts short because Scottie yells, "Stay cool, dude. Just swim."

Wait, what? I sit up quickly as Eleanor does the same. "What's going on?"

"Someone yelled shark." Moonbeam shrugs as we start scouring the water.

Or they do because I'm already speed-walking toward the shoreline, taking inventory.

Where are they?

TJ. Yes. I take a breath, head shifting, heart calming. *And Nate.*

"Dude, you're fine," Scottie yells again. "It's not a shark."

Whoever he's yelling at can't hear him because they're flailing in the water, kicking up a shower around them.

And then I see it.

Chad's waist-high in the water, falling down, flinging his arms around, trying to swim. Basically, drowning himself as he tries to run out.

"Just stand up," Scottie yells.

But to no avail, because it's like he's trying to stop, drop, and roll to the wrong disaster. TJ and Nate stroll out, boards under their arms, just as Crew joins us.

I'm staring up at them, their eyes gleaming with trouble, smirks on their faces.

"Shark?"

"Dolphins," TJ says back before dipping and kissing me right on the lips.

The boards are stuck in the sand before they turn, and we stand there watching Chad crawl out on his hands and knees, waterlogged, dramatically gasping, still yelling, "Help," and "Shark."

The surf instructors scramble to his aide, dragging him the rest of way, each with a hand under his arm and on his wrist.

Oh my god. Stop.

I squeal, hiding my face in Nate's arm as Chad drops to his knees and Moonbeam runs to him.

"Are you okay?" she rushes out, pulling his scuba head off and unzipping the suit. "You need to breathe, lover."

But as she does, she blanches, covering her mouth. Then dry heaves. Loudly.

The sound punctuates the space.

"Oh my god. What's that smell?"

Nate grabs my waist, and TJ whispers, "Noooo," like two kids that can't believe they're about to open the present they've been waiting for.

I'm blinking, expecting but *not* expecting what's coming next.

"There was a shark," he shouts, and I start to laugh, covering my mouth. "I thought I was going to die." He looks panicked. Moonbeam dry heaves again. "They said shark."

TJ holds up his hands, shrugging. "Sorry, man. Just some dolphins."

Chad starts to stand, his hand shooting behind him to his ass. And that's when it happens.

Eleanor scream-laughs. "Did you shit your pants?"

She looks at me, shaking my shoulders, making my whole body move, but I can't speak because my eyes are full of tears.

"Millie. He shit his pants!"

"That's right up the back," TJ confers with the guys, who just nod back. "They're gonna have to take a hose to him."

"I thought I was going to die," he screams, walking wide-legged up the beach before yelling, "Moon," over his shoulder.

She lingers with Scottie before running after her shitty boyfriend. And the five of us stand on the beach, laughing harder than we ever have.

Eleanor throws her arm over my shoulder, looking me in the eyes.

"Mills, I change my mind. Don't ever take that necklace off. It's the best good-luck charm you've ever received."

twenty

. . .

"Let's remember that he shit his own pants."

millie

"**C**an we all agree we're bailing on this mission?" Eleanor jokes, raising her eyebrows at me. "This girl needs a margarita and a nap."

I chuckle, nodding, because for the last hour, TJ's had us hunting for some waterfall he overheard some people talking about at the breakfast buffet.

However, I'm starting to think it's not even on this island.

Although I'm not really complaining because riding with my arms wrapped around him as he zoomed around at top speed has been basically perfect.

I'd say the ride of my life, but the guys delivered that last night.

Speaking of guys, Nate's already pawing at me, trying to coax me off my pink moped and onto his.

I laugh. "Stop."

"It's my turn. He's had you for over an hour."

The smile on my face won't go away as I switch, sitting in front of him. Because they've been doing this all day. It was rock paper scissors for who got to drive me when we started out. TJ won.

And when we stopped at a popular spot at the beach to take some pictures, I became the willing victim of a kidnapping, ending up on the back of Nate's pink moped.

I love that they're pink. It's so funny to see these behemoth men puttering around, rocking out to eighties rock music. TJ, Crew, and Nate singing "Pour Some Sugar On Me" by Def Leppard will go down as the karaoke boy band the world needs.

Still, I'm not buying that the company didn't have an extra moped for me.

These boys are full of lies. Deliciously selfish, sexy lies.

"I think this might be one of my favorite days here," I say aloud to nobody in particular. "Besides the fact that we've been on a wild goose chase."

The breeze blows like it's a paid actor as I let my baby blue helmet dangle in my hand.

Nate plants another kiss on my forehead, grinning. "Oh yeah, why? Because Chad canceled, shamed into hiding?"

I chuckle, leaning sideways, making Nate hold me up so I can twist enough to look at him.

But Eleanor beats me to the punch, chiming in, "Let's remember that he shit his own pants. He brought shame upon his own house."

I right myself, shrugging and talking over my shoulder. "Not everything's about Chad. I don't know...it just feels lighter today. Easy. Fun. Maybe, yeah, partly because

DJ Dookie isn't here, but also because I like hanging out with you guys."

That was more honesty than I knew I was going to share. But I do like hanging with them, and what Eleanor said yesterday stuck. *"They like you."*

Nate's nodding, staring at me. There's something about it...the way he's looking. It feels like he has something to say, so I smile.

But whatever it was is fleeting because he looks away as TJ laughs.

The guys walk out of the store, holding up bags. Eleanor cheers just as TJ sets his sights on me.

"No way," he barks playfully. "You stole my girl. Give her back."

Nate chuckles. "Bullshit. She's been on your moped for the last hour. It's my turn."

Anybody who says two guys fighting over you is toxic, is wrong and a hater. I'm starting to love when they do this.

Honestly, outside of bed is almost as satisfying as inside. *Almost*, because no matter how much they vied for my attention today, it'll never trump the way Nate first told me to wait to orgasm with him as TJ told me I had to beg for one.

I laugh, sliding off Nate's moped as he frowns grumpily. So I press my lips together to hide my smile before I look between them.

"I've said this before, and I'll say it again...for two people who live a certain lifestyle, you're terrible at sharing."

TJ narrows his eyes on me, looking way too fucking cute as he hands me a box of Hot Tamales.

"Smalls, there's an empty bathroom we can use to prove that theory wrong if you want."

Nate grabs my hips, pulling me backward and closer to him just as TJ pounces, nuzzling my neck, making me squeal with laughter.

Eleanor makes a dry heave sound, and I laugh as Crew hands her candy.

"I can't believe I'm witnessing a miracle. Never did I ever think my dumbass best friends would ever end up with the same girl. Way to lock 'em down, Mills."

"Whoa, whoa, whoa," Nate throws out as TJ shakes his head.

Meanwhile, my eyes nearly pop out of my head as I semi-choke on my Hot Tamales, spitting out my words. "We're just having fun. Right?" I look at the guys, TJ pointing at me in agreement. "There's no locking anyone up happening over here. Or down or whatever."

"Exactly," Nate adds.

I cut in again. "They don't even date the girls they bang. Duh."

My forehead scrunches, immediately embarrassed by my insinuative overshare. So I pop a few more Hot Tamales in my mouth.

Eleanor grins, putting her helmet on. "Okay, well… now that we have that all cleared up. If you super-platonic friends who fuck are ready to head back…"

The handful of candy I'm holding flies at her as she laughs, and Crew acts like he's mortally injured when it hits them. I roll my eyes as I put my helmet on, enjoying the feel of Nate's arms engulfing me as he starts our pink moped.

"Ready, friend?" he jokes, and I smile.

"Yes, pal. Let's go."

Elle: Hear me out....

I LOOK UP FROM FREDDIE THE FLOATIE, ACCEPTING A CAN OF margarita from TJ. Not having a minibar sucks.

Me: No.

I can almost hear her laugh.

Elle: What if they did?

Me: They don't. So there's no point to your point.

Elle: All I'm saying is what's the harm in seeing where it goes?

We're not real. I mean, we are...but we aren't.

What she sees is the version of us we're selling. Even though we almost exposed ourselves this afternoon.

I thought I was going to have a heart attack when they said I locked them down. Shit, they almost did too. Which is weird because we should've been congratulating ourselves on our acting skills. Registering for fucking SAG cards and setting up Hollywood auditions.

This is not real.

But that's the part that's continually fucking with my head. Because I think they do actually like me.

Still though, we can like each other and not want to explore anything other than Thursday through Sunday. And I remember what TJ said the other day back at the beach: *"Pussy's one thing, someone's heart is different."*

Problem is. She's fucking right. I do like them. A lot.
But I'm not admitting that to her. Not right now.

> Me: What are you wearing tonight?

> Elle: Disappointment. Because my bestie is a chicken shit.

I snort-laugh, glancing up at the guys, who are both
looking at me. "Eleanor," I offer with a wave of my phone
before looking back down.

> Me: Cool. I was going to wear a yellow dress but now that feels too on the nose.

> Elle: hahahahahha. Just promise me you'll consider going after something you want Mills. Don't let one shitty moment make it so you never take a chance again.

> Me: Fine. Just shut up already.

> Elle: *emoji with zipper mouth.

I take a deep breath, looking up. "I'm gonna jump in
the shower."

Without even looking at me, they both stand, Nate
reaching down for my hand to help me up.

My forehead scrunches. "Do you guys need the bathroom first?"

TJ draws his head back. "Girlie. We're coming too."

I laugh, shaking my head and walking past them. "No
way. The last time we all did the shower thing, I was
stuck between you, freezing my ass off."

Nate smacks my ass, making me yelp. "Baby. You're
not showering without us."

166

I spin around, hands on my hips as I stare up at them. "The hell I'm not."

NATE GROWLS, AND I SMILE, ROLLING MY EYES.

"Stop harassing me," I tease before pointing at them. "I let you in here, didn't I? So, stay there and watch. But no touching. At. All."

TJ's eyes close as he sucks in an irritated breath before saying, "I hate Chad so much." He looks at Nate. "You know there's a big-ass shower in that room. We coulda been…" The rest comes out as a groan, making me laugh again.

I suds up the washcloth, scrubbing it over my body and showering like a normal person. I ignore the fact that water is getting everywhere since the curtain is wide open.

But the moment I run the washcloth down over my leg, Nate clears his throat, calling my eyes.

"Slower," he levels suddenly, making everything feel quiet by the way he's looking at me.

I suck some water off my bottom lip, glued to his gaze, my chest already rising faster as I glance at TJ, who cocks his head and winks.

Fuck, they're so hot. And they have been very good boys for the last three minutes. So I guess a reward is appropriate.

I stand, bringing the cloth up to my stomach and gliding it slowly around my belly button.

Their eyes never leave me. They're focused. Zeroed in. Like I'm the only fucking thing that exists.

The grip they have on the counter behind them is so hard their thick knuckles turn white.

So I keep going, sliding it up to my breast and giving my nipples more attention than needed before following a trail up my neck, letting out a sigh as I do.

TJ half blinks, like he's drunk on me. His hand drops down over his hardening cock, rubbing himself through the fabric of his basketball shorts.

I lick my lips, letting my head fall back, cleaning my throat up to my jawline before diving back between my tits.

I'm taking my time, letting them watch. And enjoying it.

Nate rocks forward like he's going to push off and attack, but I shake my head, making his eyes narrow.

"No. Touching. Nathan."

With a smirk, I bring the cloth to the water, rinsing it before I wring the water over my chest.

Teasing and torturing them might very well be my favorite hobby. I've never felt so beautiful and so fucking wanted before in my whole life.

TJ's head falls back with a groan, but I continue with our game.

My fingers curl around the washcloth as I run it down over my hip before I slide my hand directly over my pussy, letting out a gasp.

"Fuck," TJ exhales roughly.

I moan as my hips press forward, my finger rubbing myself in slow circles over the washcloth.

"You wanted me to clean every single part…right?"

I don't wait for an answer as my mouth falls open. Softer whimpers follow, and I bring my other hand to my chest, palming my breast, arching my back.

"Smalls." TJ says my name like a warning, but I don't stop.

The need has taken over. I don't want to. I'm going to come and make them watch.

But well-laid plans and all because I look over at them just as they reach over their shoulders and drag their T-shirts off. Neither hesitates to toss their shirts to the side before shorts come off next.

"Get out," Nate demands, fisting his cock. "Right fucking now."

I don't move, immediately wetter.

"You said no touching," TJ grits. "So we won't touch." He points to the ground a hundred times in a row. "Get the fuck out."

I smirk. This is too much fun. The time I take shutting off the water makes TJ crack his neck twice. And when I say, "Towel, please," looking between them, I have to try like hell not to laugh. Because Nate's jaw looks like it's strained harder than his dick.

He still holds it open for me though.

My teeth scrape my bottom lip as I look up at them, tucking the front in around my chest.

"Okay...I'm out," I say with a challenge lacing my words. "If you're fucking me, you have to do it without touching me. Excited to see what you come up with."

The sound the door makes slamming open for me makes my shoulders jump.

"Is that a challenge, Scrappy?" Nate levels, looking over at TJ when I nod.

TJ chuckles, leaning down to my ear. "You dirty little bitch. You're on. Get the fuck in the room."

My pussy says, "Yes, sir," before I do.

I'm ushered out of the foggy bathroom by their words

and into the bedroom before my towel is torn from my body.

Nate stands in front of me, his intense gaze piercing right through me.

"Get on your knees," he offers arrogantly.

The shiver that racks my body is unmissable. But he holds my eyes as I use the end of the bed to help lower me to the ground, my hands automatically coming to his thighs.

"The rules don't apply to me...to be clear. I'll touch whatever I want."

Nate strokes his gorgeous cock in front of my face slowly, dragging his hand to the very top before tugging down.

"Get it wet."

I spit on his cock without warning.

His shoulders shake as he uses it, spinning his hand around. "You look good bad. But I'm gonna fuck that mouth until you're pleading to be good."

My mouth is watering, pussy dripping.

TJ's voice calls to me. "Spread your legs. Put those fingers back in that pretty pussy."

I suck in a breath, ghosting my fingertips over my body, down my stomach, and straight into my wetness.

"Let Daddy taste," he croons, motioning with two fingers for my hand.

I obey and lift my hand, watching TJ lick me off before I exhale harshly. "You know you're breaking the rules, right?"

"I've never been one to follow 'em. But I'm not fucking you, so technically I can touch you.'"

Before I can say anything, TJ grips the back of my hair. "Now, open and suck him good, baby."

My body's already begging, so fucking turned on because Nate's staring down as TJ controls my head, fucking Nate with my mouth.

Nate exhales a deep, appreciative groan, and my body contracts, but TJ bobs my head forward again.

"That's it. Swallow him back."

I feel Nate hit my throat before TJ pulls me back.

"Fuck yourself," Nate growls before TJ forces me forward again, letting me swallow more of Nate.

I'm lost. Completely fucking spun.

My eyes roll back as I try and concentrate on my clit, but TJ drags me off Nate's cock without warning and directly onto his.

I gasp as he thrusts his hard cock inside my mouth, but it turns into a moan against his shaft.

"You love that dick, Millie? You want to swallow our cum, don't you? Let us cover your face. Me *and* Nate. I'll fucking put it down your throat. And Nate can smear it on your chin. Maybe we'll let it drip over your tits."

Nate growls, finishing TJ's words, "Because you're our whore. Tell us, baby."

My hand moves faster and faster over my swollen clit, barely able to keep pace as they switch again.

Leaving me breathing hard for only enough time to say, "Yes. I'm your whore."

Nate takes over, grabbing my hair himself, fucking my mouth without tenderness, grunting as he hits the back of my throat.

"Your mouth is so fucking sweet. But I want these lips bruised."

Oh god. I want to come. I need to.

My hand falters, falling away from my clit. TJ growls, tugging me away, palming the top of my head as he takes a turn hammering inside my hollowed cheeks.

"You better fuck yourself. Rub that fucking clit now."

His voice is strained, and the way he's fucking my mouth is making my whole body move. It's relentless and rough. There's nothing gentle about it.

It's pure, unadulterated bliss.

My eyes water, and he grips and regrips the sides of my head, fucking my mouth like he could die and be happy.

"Oh fuck. Millie. Fuck me so good. That's it, make Daddy come, baby." He groans alongside the wet sounds of Nate jerking himself next to my face.

I'm fingering myself desperately. So fucking needy. I want them.

Everywhere.

Nate shoves TJ off me, tugging my chin and barking, "Suck."

And I think I've arrived in heaven. I'm being torn apart by two men who can't get enough of me.

Nate's breath is stuttered, mirroring TJ's, and it's all I can hear. All I can focus on. I'm sucking Nate off, hollowing my cheeks as hard as I can as TJ jerks himself off.

Both of their hands are in my hair.

My fingers move between my thighs, but I can't focus. I just want to make them come. Taste their cum on my lips and in my mouth.

I've never felt like this. My body is climbing, then receding, before climbing again. It's torture and heaven all in one. I moan as if I'm coming, knowing it'll throw them over the edge.

"Baby. Oh fuck," Nate groans loudly. "I'm coming. Swallow it. Swallow for me."

I do as he pulls his cock almost out of my mouth before warm spurts of saltiness grace my tongue, filling my mouth.

"Yes. Yes. Yes. Open your fucking mouth," TJ grits out as Nate pulls out.

TJ's cum hits my lips before joining Nate's, coating the inside of my mouth as I swallow.

I shudder, feeling impossibly explosive, tasting them together.

My eyes close as I breathe hard, feeling one of them swipe what's left on my chin back inside my mouth. I suck it off the pad of their finger before sitting back on my haunches.

"You're fucking beautiful," Nate levels.

I blink open, smiling up at him before they each extend a hand and help me up. TJ leans down and kisses me before Nate does the same.

"I think I need another shower." I laugh, but they shake their heads. "Fine, I'll be wanton hussy all night."

Nate smacks my ass as he heads toward the bathroom, but TJ wraps me in a hug. So I wrap my arms around him, but the second I do, he lifts me off the ground, guiding my legs around him, making me laugh. He just holds me for a minute before his head draws back, and he stares into my eyes.

"Yo—"

"Yo, ho," I answer back like a sexy pirate, but I'm set to my feet.

He looks down at his stomach, then at my pussy. "Where is it?"

I swallow, knowing exactly what he just figured out.

Shit. I'm grinning before grabbing my underwear and dress that was waiting for me on the bed.

"Where's what?" I say like the liar I am.

But how do I explain that I was just really into them coming and couldn't focus? Because I'm pretty sure they won't let me leave the damn room until I've mastered the skill. I'm halfway to sliding on my panties as TJ's words make me freeze.

"You...where's the fucking mess that juicy pussy makes?"

Oh my god. I hurry my dress over my head and shrug, trying not to laugh at his stunned face. Yep. They're going to kill me. My ass will definitely be red.

"Did you just fucking fake it?" He turns in a whole circle like he doesn't even know what to do with himself before he repeats himself without a question mark at the end. "You faked it."

"The thing is—" I start, but his brows hit his forehead.

I'm already slipping on my shoes as he stalks the four steps to open the bathroom door, yelling to Nate.

"She faked it." He pats his stomach where my bare pussy was just hanging out, "There's no mess. I just picked her up, and there was no mess."

I hear the shampoo or whatever Nate had in his hand hit the bathtub floor.

The hair tie around my wrist has never tied my hair in a ponytail faster. And by the time TJ's turned around, I'm halfway out the bedroom door.

"You guys hurry, okay? I'll meet you downstairs."

The last thing I hear is my name bellowed through the fourteen total square feet we're housed.

But people always say you should "leave 'em wanting more." And I'm pretty sure the guys want it all.

twenty-one

. . .

"It doesn't matter where you come. Just as long as you're screaming our names."

tweedles

tj

Nate and I are staring across the table at her.

We look like we're sitting at the kids' table because our asses are planted on stools too close to the ground, hiking our knees up way too high. And like a bunch of kids forced to be at a party they don't want to be at, Nate and I aren't just wearing leis around our necks. We've accessorized with scowls on our faces.

I let out another heavy breath, making Crew look at me.

He's stuck between us because the girls wanted to be next to each other, only adding to our frustration.

My teeth grind, thinking about how that little vixen hightailed right out the door and made it impossible to teach her a lesson.

And now I can't even enjoy my poi. *Poi, poi me.*

"Hey, look at this." Crew hands me a flyer for a Valentine's costume party the hotel's having on Sunday. Our last night here. But I don't care.

I toss it back on the table, looking at him for a minute before I take a deep breath.

"Your shirt's dumb."

He looks down at himself, yelling, "I didn't fucking ask," filled with humor.

He picks the paper up and hands it to Eleanor across the table as he keeps speaking. "And my girl got it for me, so fuck you, loser. Did your girl get you a shirt with fake abs spray-painted on it? Ummm, no."

No. The only thing my girl did was fake her orgasm and ignore my grumpy face.

I'm pissed but also compelled to make her come. Real fucking hard. So, I can't really be pissed. It's more like I'm aggressively motivated. And grumpy as hell.

Nate and I lean back into our chairs at the same time, still staring at her. I shift my head, locking eyes with him, and I can tell he's thinking the same as me.

Crew leans back too, trying to join in, his fingers interlocked behind his head, but we push him forward at the same time. The silverware clatters when his hands stop his movement.

"For fuck's sake," he laughs. "What the hell did you do to them, Mills? Because I think you might've broken them."

She laughs, and we whip our heads back to hers, glaring.

"They're fine," she teases, giving me a wink.

But I growl, and Nate throws out, "Nope. We're not fine...until Millie's making a goddamn mess."

She picks up a piece of pineapple, hiding her laughter since everyone is looking at us like they're confused. But that still doesn't stop her from batting her lashes.

We aren't amused.

I mean, we are, but it's not fair.

We make her come. That's it. Period. End of sentence.

And she cheated.

Now she's going to pay for it.

I just haven't figured out how to out-supervillain a villain.

"Stop pouting," she teases, tossing her pineapple rind at me across the table, making Eleanor and Crew volley between the three of us for context clues. "There's always tomorrow for me to strive for a mess."

Nate crosses his arms, and she giggles harder, holding up the flyer. "PS, I think I know what we should go as."

Before I can think of something snappy to say, fire lights the sky as a traditional Samoan fire dance begins, accompanied by Hawaiian hula dancers.

Everyone's attention turns to the show, but mine's still on Millie. Nate shoves Crew forward again, leaning over his back.

"I say we just grab her and go. Fuck it."

I raise my brows, considering what he's said. "Just grab her? Like over a shoulder? Cuz she ain't gonna leave otherwise."

He nods, but Crew fights back, sitting between us, looking back and forth. Nobody can hear us anymore with all the music, so he smiles.

"Something happened, and I don't think I wanna know what. But...if a grab and smash is needed, I'll help. So long as you two idiots stop pushing me around. I'm supposed to get beat up by opposing teams only, dicks."

We smile as he scoots his tiny stool back from the long table, making tiny little hops before he has enough room to stand.

"Watch for my signal," he throws out.

Nate and I look at each other because what signal? *What the fuck is he doing?*

The deep thrum of bass that comes from the drums makes my chest rumble, but I'm watching, my eyes following Crew as he walks around the table.

Nate's tapping me, feeling the same anticipation because that's the best thing about our best friend. He's unpredictable. You have to be to marry a whole-ass stranger on a whim in Vegas.

He looks over at us, chuckling to himself before stopping and waiting behind a waiter Millie's stopped. She's peppering him with questions about the traditions and meanings of the dances being done.

"Beautiful," she breathes in response to something he explains, and I can't help myself—I smile.

"What's he doing?" Nate breathes, but I don't look at him as I shake my head because I don't know either.

Crew discreetly motions for us to get up, so we start scooting our tiny stools out like two jackasses just as he leans down and says something to Millie.

She nods and rises to her feet, completely unaware of what we're doing. But Crew looks at her with a double-agent kind of grin on his face.

"Sorry, buddy. But I have to turn you over," he shouts, and her head swings in our direction.

Her eyes light up, and she squeals as Crew cups his hands under her armpits, lifting Millie straight into the air and passing that girl right over the table.

Nate laughs loudly, as do I, because the shock on her

face is something else.

Her feet land on my stool, bringing us eye to eye.

She smiles, so I kiss her lips, quickly saying, "Time to go, Smalls," before I dip a shoulder and toss her lying ass right over it.

Crew and Eleanor break out into applause as Nate lifts her hair from her face. "Say good night, Scrappy."

"Good night," she shouts, smacking my ass a hundred times.

I'm laughing with Nate behind me as we walk the pathway between the tables, section after section also applauding as we pass.

My eyes scan the doors, noticing they're all shut. But there has to be a way back in, so I keep looking, hearing the music growing louder behind us.

Nate must be wondering, too, because he calls out from behind, "Over there. On your right."

I nod, giving Millie a pop up, adjusting her on my shoulder and making her squeal as we head about twenty feet to the damn promised land.

She's still pretending to put up a fight, laughing and threatening us playfully, but she's just as excited as we are to get her back to the fucking room.

I swear, if she ever fakes that shit again… No. Not on my watch.

"Smalls, keep it up," I tease, "because you're gonna pay for being a brat."

She laughs. So to drive home my point, I nip at her hip. The smirk on my face is permanent because the way she squirms tells me she liked that a lot.

Goddamn, the shit I want to do to her right now.

I'm lost in that thought as I round through the exit when I hear, "Whoa, whoa, whoa."

179

Nate's voice echoes behind me, screeching us to a halt. Because in the blink of an eye, the music changed, and the doorway we were heading through is littered with performers, all filing out and around us, forcing all of us backward as we get caught up in the fray.

"What the fuck?" I spin around with Millie shrieking, bumping into Nate, who's laughing.

We're shuffling and stumbling over each other because a million people in headdresses and bright costumes are coming out of the woodwork.

We're fucking surrounded.

Millie's pushing off my hips, presumably looking around before I hear her say, "Holy shit?" before she starts throwing out compliments and apologies to strangers as they ignore us, clearly focused on the task at hand.

What once was a mission into the hotel has now become one out of this crowd. But we're failing. Because I can't stop the wave of people pushing us toward the stage.

And the closer we get, the harder I'm laughing. *Oh shit.*

She's beating my ass like a drum because she knows it too.

"Jesus," Nate shouts, looking at me as I die, laughing harder.

I swear to god, any other crowd of people, Nate and I could slice through like butter. But these dudes....they're all our size. Where's the recruiter at when we need him?

Fuck, we got nothing on these dudes.

Nate's got me by the front of my shirt, trying to shoulder his way through everyone, but it's no use.

"TJ," Millie shouts, hitting my back again. "Are we

headed onstage?"

I don't want to say yes, but....*yeah.*

We're pushed and shoved, sent up two steps until, like something out of a fucking movie, we are indeed standing on the stage.

If we weren't a spectacle before, we certainly are now.

The music breaks, growing quiet as a spotlight suddenly shines down.

"I'm going to die," she groans against my back as an entire Māori Haka group files out around us. "The entire hotel is staring at my ass."

"But it's a nice one," I laugh.

The crowd goes wild. We even see Eleanor and Crew stand and clap.

So, we do what anyone would do in this situation. Nate gives a wave, and I nod my head and turn so Millie can take her bow too, so to speak.

She's never going to forgive us.

As soon as the chants begin, Nate and I take a few steps back before we pivot and finally disappear out of sight, down the steps of the back of the stage.

We move at a clip because the faster we get out of Dodge, the better.

"Where are we going now?" she breathes out the moment we hit darkness, finally clearing out of the party and away from people. "A couple more luaus down the beach? I'm going to kill you."

I laugh, loud and hard, just as my feet hit the sand.

"You're gonna kill us? We're about to murder that pussy."

Nate chimes in. "Who needs a bed when you got a beach? Cuz, baby, it doesn't matter where you come. Just as long as you're screaming our names."

twenty-two

. . .

"Let's stay on this beach forever."

millie

We're on the beach, darkness bleeding out everywhere, far enough away that only faint sounds of the luau mix with the waves crashing onto the shore.

"Now," TJ levels, setting me to my feet, the humor once gracing his words gone. "As punishment for lying, *we* are going to make you come."

I brush my hair out of my face, looking up between their moonlit faces, still unbelieving at what just happened but very much willing to keep playing along.

Because, to be honest, that display of caveman buffoonery was kind of hot. The whole Four Seasons world just saw me over his shoulder, Nate in tow.

It's the equivalent of *I licked them, so they're mine.*

My voice fills with faux fear as I raise my hands to my cheeks.

"Oh no...don't punish me. How will I survive?"

Nate pushes my hand out of the way, cradling my chin and pulling my eyes to his. The familiar crackling ignites as he licks his bottom lip before leaning down so we're eye to eye.

"We're gonna make you come until you can't walk, baby. As many times as it takes to ensure you never fucking try and lie to us again."

Oh. There's a lot in that sentence. And it's all making me very wet. But instead of saying anything back, I put my hands on his massive shoulders and kiss him.

Bring it on.

His lips are warm and soft as they glide over mine, tasting and indulging.

TJ's body heat engulfs my back just as Nate's tongue dives inside my mouth, and our heads tilt as they dance. It's teasing and slow.

And it's making me press my tits into his chest.

TJ's hands slide up the sides of my body, taking my dress with it just a little before his fingers tickle my neck and weave into my hair. He lifts the end of my pony before pressing a kiss against my shoulder.

Nobody can see us out here, but it still feels danger-ous. And the idea that we could be caught in filthy acts makes my clit throb.

"Baby, don't ever fucking deprive us again," Nate levels against my lips.

TJ kisses across my back, adding, "Making you come is the whole point. That's what gets us off. It's knowing that we take you somewhere that nobody else can."

I'm shivering because even though they didn't say anything dirty, it's still the hottest thing I've ever heard.

Men who like to please...huh. I've heard the lore, but I

thought it was like hearing about a narwhal. They exist. I've just never seen one.

"Okay," I say on an exhale as TJ's hands melt over my breasts, "never again. Promise."

Nate skims his fingertips down over my dress, biting my bottom lip gently as he cups my pussy. The deep bass of his voice fills my ears, doing dirty things to my body.

"I'm gonna finger you. Eat you. Then fuck you twice. In that order."

Holy shit. I'm already ruined.

I seal my lips to Nate's neck, my body writhing between the feel of these men. He groans against the pressure of my lips, tilting his head, making room for me to kiss and suck his skin. Something about it makes me want to leave a mark.

Let everyone see I've been here.

TJ urges my legs open, kicking them gently just as Nate bunches my dress, slowly curling his fingers around the fabric inch by inch.

I swallow hard, already breathless.

"I want you," I breathe out, knowing they understand I mean both of them.

Nate's fingers duck under what he's lifted, tickling my clit and making me gasp.

"Fuck. You're so wet. I can feel it through your panties," Nate growls.

This feels so dirty. TJ trailing kisses over my shoulders. My dress lifted enough to expose me as Nate swipes his fingers back and forth over my covered clit, letting the wetness bleed through the fabric.

TJ pinches one of my nipples, and I whimper, seeing Nate's jaw tense before he swipes my thong to the side and thrusts his middle finger inside me.

Jesus. My body and mind are fucking reeling because Nate's so possessed with the need to make me come that he can't be bothered to even take my panties off.

His palm rubs my clit as he begins slowly fucking me. Our eyes lock, and my lips part.

I can hear how wet I am. The crude sound makes TJ grind his hard cock against my ass. My fingers curl around Nate's shirt, holding on for support because I'm immediately overwhelmed by the sensation of being finger fucked.

Nate's looking at me, but he's speaking over my shoulder, and it feels fucking exactly the right amount of degrading.

"Her pussy is fucking dripping like a good little slut."

My eyes flutter as I listen to how he's speaking about me.

TJ's hand kneads my ass harshly. "Lemme see."

I brace myself, waiting for Nate to pull his finger out so that TJ can take his turn. But that's not what happens.

TJ's hand rounds my ass, coming up from behind, and pushes inside me.

With Nate.

They're *both* inside of me, fucking my cunt together.

TJ's breath is warm on the back of my neck. "Oh fuck. She likes that. You feel her used little cunt squeeze?"

"Fuck yeah, she does. That pussy's clenching so hard around us."

My stomach tightens as they fuck me in unison, thrusting in and out. In and out. Faster and faster.

Nate's palm rubs my clit at the same time, creating the perfect amount of friction to make my hips thrust and circle.

"Yes. Oh my god. Don't stop. Please."

TJ's thumb angles, and I feel pressure there. He's rubbing my asshole. The sensation is mind-splitting. Nate at my clit and TJ at my ass.

"Oh fuck. That feels so good. Make me come. Please. I'm sorry I lied."

Nate's mouth seals over mine, kissing me roughly as their fingers stretch me. He hums, "Mmhmm," into my mouth as TJ licks up the back of my neck and bites gently at the skin.

Jesus Christ. They're animals.

"That's it, baby. Come on our fingers. I can feel your body begging for it."

He's right. My body is begging for it.

My legs are spread, one hand on Nate's chest and the other one reaching down behind me, holding on to TJ's shorts. I'm sandwiched between them, our bodies swaying together for anyone to see as their fingers glide in and out of my slickness, driving deeper and deeper.

Waves crash louder as my body hums and shudders.

Because they're kissing me. Free hands run over my body as I feel my need rise higher and higher.

"Please, please, please, please," I start to chant, holding them tighter.

The feeling starts in my stomach, spreading downward, making me press my hips forward harder and grind into Nate's hand.

I'm panting, whimpering, my eyes squeezed shut because I want it so bad. I want to come so badly that I feel crazed. As if nothing else matters.

"Do you feel that?" Nate whispers to TJ, whose voice is dangerously low and sexy as he answers, "Yeah…come on, baby. Come for us. Let us feel that pussy explode and drip all over our hands."

I'm breathing harder and harder, grinding into their fingers, whimpering as my head falls back onto TJ's chest.

"Yes, fuck…. yes, yes, yes."

Everything inside of me locks up before I combust, coming so hard it feels like it's knocked the wind out of me.

But it hasn't because TJ's hand gently covers my mouth as I scream. My whole body quivers—even my pelvis shakes as my body shatters.

My knees suddenly give, but Nate holds me up, his strong arm wrapped around me, both their fingers still inside me.

My hands come to TJ's wrist, gripping it because they're starting again. They're not stopping. I slap at TJ's hand, but he whispers in my ear.

"No, Smalls. You're not done. Ride it out, baby. That pussy's coming for us again."

I can't take it. I'm too sensitive. Everywhere. But that doesn't stop their fingers from fighting for space inside me, fucking me in a punishing rhythm as they thrust in and out.

"I can't," I breathe through a space between TJ's fingers, still unable to open my eyes. "Nate. TJ. I can't. It's too much…I won't be able—"

My words are cut off because the feeling takes over, keeping me in a fucking chokehold.

"Goddammit," Nate growls, locking his hand around my throat. "You fucking come again for us."

I'm shaking my head, but my pussy is obeying, listening to its owners. It won't say no to them.

They're relentless, unwavering in their pursuit as another orgasm hits me so hard that I bite TJ's palm.

He hisses against my neck, sealing his lips to the soft skin and sucking. It's animalistic. But we're heathens.

"Oh fuck," Nate groans. "She's squirting."

I gasp, suddenly sucking in a breath so hard it makes my body catapult forward and bend over because their fingers leave me at the same time, abandoning my fucked cunt as they drop to their knees, eating my cum off me.

Nate's tongue laps over my clit, his hands painfully gripping my waist as TJ licks me from ass to hole, diving inside me, circling before devouring the rest.

My fingers gently stroke Nate's hair as they clean my thighs, my pussy, my ass cheeks. Every piece of me, whispering praises into my skin.

"You're fucking perfect." … "This pussy is beautiful used."

I can barely function. My vision is still blurred as I breathe slower and slower, feeling my heart beating out of my chest.

I walk my hands up Nate's back so I'm upright again, taking another deep breath.

Nate sits back, his jaw slack, glistening in the moonlight, covered in me. TJ's heavy breaths come from behind as he wraps his arms around my waist, and I feel his chest rising and falling.

I lick my lips before smiling. "Let's stay on this beach forever."

It's Nate's voice that makes me quiver again.

"Done. Because that was one down. We still have three to go."

twenty-three

. . .

"How about room service and I'm dessert?"

tweedles

nate

TJ and I have been lying here on either side of her since the sun peeked out from the horizon. Neither of us has said a word. We're just staring at her, occasionally glancing at each other.

Because we both know we're fucked.

"Teej," I finally break, but he whispers back with a grin, "Shh... you'll wake the baby."

He holds up his phone, so I grab mine too, which thankfully has three percent battery. I'm waiting as he types, eyes falling on her again, watching her breathe and smiling because she doesn't snore—she purrs.

My phone vibrates, tearing me away, so I swipe it open.

TJ: We got a problem. You feel me?

Me: Yeah. A fucking big one.

I see him nod his head before he types quickly.

TJ: This is something we've never done. I mean the shit last night, bro.

My brows draw together.

Me: I know.

TJ: She's fucking different, Nate. She handles us like it's second nature. And that's fucking with my head.

This time, it's me nodding my head. But he texts again.

TJ: Admit it though. You're fucking into her too.

I look up, not wanting to answer. Because once I say it, I know I'm done. We're done. There's no closing Pandora's box.

TJ stares at me, searching my eyes, but I look down at my phone.

The thing is, he's right. Millie never seems to feel suffocated or torn between us. She likes that we fight for space inside her. In more ways than one. And honestly, last night, I liked watching her come.

No matter who was the cause.

My fingers click against the keys, halting when she sighs and rolls over. I hold my breath until she starts purring again before I start typing.

> Me: Doesn't matter. She was clear from the start. She's only fucking with us because we're no commitment.

> TJ: Joke's on her. I've been catching feelings since like day three. I'm gonna text my sisters and ask what they do for shit like this.

> Me: Do not text them.

> TJ: Or maybe...hear me out. We should start playing Cuffing Season real low everywhere we go. Like subliminal messaging.

I laugh then catch myself, watching him turn away so he won't either.

We're so fucked. Two Romeos without a Juliet.

Millie's arms stretch above her head as she lets out a big yawn before fluttering her lashes open and smiling back and forth between us.

"You know," she says, all raspy and fucking adorable. "These stolen pool rafts are actually quite comfortable, but I can't help but feel like we're cheating on Freddie."

I laugh, pocketing my phone and glancing at TJ, who's doing the same. Our secret conversation is tabled.

He grabs her waist, moving her hair to admire the mark he left on her neck before he taps her nose.

"How about we get you upstairs and wake you up properly?"

"Best idea ever," she whispers.

What would this look like? Past Sunday, past a month from now.

The thought has my pulse picking up speed. Because despite all my disagreeing, I can't help but really fucking like the way he makes her smile as her hand finds mine and tucks inside.

Fuck. I really like the girl.

tj

"Fuck me," she breathes, sweat glistening on the back of her neck.

I lick it, dragging my tongue up her skin before kissing the damp spot. Fucking her is all I want to do. We're not leaving this room today.

I wrap my arms around her, hugging her tight to me, her back to my chest.

Jesus. My dick's seated so deep in her ass that it's hard to concentrate on anything else. And all I can hear is my own breath panted back against my lips, which are sealed against her back.

She's writhing between both of us, riding us at the same time.

Nate in her pussy, me in her ass.

Goddamn. How the fuck are we supposed to live without this at the end of the week?

"Come, baby," Nate growls, taking her mouth again.

Her hands grip his shoulders as we all rock together, undulating as she lifts faster and faster. Oh fuck, she's grinding over our cocks, and I feel my balls draw up.

I want her so bad. I want to come inside her.

The moans ripping between us are almost whines, each of us fucking begging for release. The smell of sex fills the room, hovering over us like a thick fog, drawing inside with each inhale.

We're lost in the moment and found in our connection. Because of her. She's the anchor. Our rock-hard dicks fill her over and over, swollen harder than they've ever been, needing to fill her.

"Come inside of me," she whispers. "Come inside of me at the same time."

My fingers weave into her hair at the nape of her neck, and I grip it mercilessly as I jut my hips up, meeting her ass, hearing it slap down against Nate.

I groan loudly as her ass contracts, squeezing my cock inside its warm walls and jerking my shaft, bringing me right over the edge.

My body tenses up as I let go, spurt after spurt filling her.

"Fuck, baby. That pussy's so good," Nate growls, coming too as she shatters around us, quivering and shaking.

She's so beautiful like this. As I think it, the words fall out.

"You're beautiful like this. Used and full. Marked by us."

I squeeze her tighter to me, my forehead on her shoulder. I'm still panting, almost unable to catch my breath. Her head falls back against mine, but I can tell she's smiling as she says, "Did I make enough of a mess this time?"

Nate chuckles as we sit there, clinging to her, peppering kisses over her shoulders and chest until our breaths finally slow down and she sighs.

"Shower? Then room service?"

Nate groans at the same time as I shake my head

against her back.

She giggles. "Okay. How about room service and I'm dessert?"

My dick pulses inside her, before I force her face to mine and I growl, "Get extra whipped cream."

twenty-four

. . .

"Not even with your help, sexual Jesus."

millie

I laugh, my cheeks hurting from smiling so much while I hold a shot glass in my hand.

TJ's cheeks are pinked by the sun as he smiles back, and I say, "Your turn."

The guys and I have been at the pool most of the day, just hanging out and relaxing, especially since after leaving the beach yesterday, we didn't really leave our bed.

Not that I'm complaining. It was perfect. But today, I'm exhausted, and my girlie downstairs needs some R&R. If I'm being honest though, so does my head because I've been living inside it, still thinking about what Eleanor said.

What if they did?

Those four words are haunting me because clearly, friends with bennies is a tried-and-true failure. Someone always ends up developing feelings. And currently, that sucker is me.

Yuck. I hate this. And that's exactly why I jumped at the idea of day drinking.

So here we are, two shots in and another to go if TJ would ever make his toast.

TJ nods, thinking before he grins.

"Okay, okay. I'm trying to remember this thing I saw on a Reddit post once—" He holds up a finger, eyebrows rising like it's coming to him before he snaps his finger and lifts the shot glass higher. "If the ocean was liquor and I was a duck, I'd dive to the bottom and drink my way up, but the ocean is water, and I'm not a duck, so let's just do these shots and all get fucked-up."

We hoot and holler like a bunch of hoodlums on a college spring break before we tap our glasses on the bar and let the tequila slide back.

I let out a breathy exhale, wincing from the sting and immediately sucking a piece of lime.

I love tequila, but it never gets easier to drink.

Nate wraps his arms around me the moment I set the glass on the bar, engulfing me in his frame and kissing my cheek three times in a row as I hug him back.

He wiggles, and I know what he's asking, so I run my nails up and down his back.

TJ motions to Crew, letting him know his drinks are ready before Nate lifts me off the ground, smirking.

"We're going back in the pool." He looks at TJ. "You coming?"

I kiss his cheek, knowing that Nate's going to jump directly into the deep end.

TJ nods, following behind us as I laugh, just dangling in his arms, my arms wrapped around his neck.

"You're cute," I whisper. "Like my very own giant teddy bear."

He chuckles, then takes a deep breath.

We get to the edge of the pool, but instead of jumping in, Nate sets me to my feet. He's staring down at me, looking deeply into my eyes with that intense stare he has before his fingers reach up to brush my hair out of my eyes.

"What? What's wrong?" I breathe out, confused by his mood change.

He shakes his head minutely, grinning. Something about it feels shy.

But I don't get time to press because I'm all but tackled directly into the pool by TJ.

We splash into the pool, and I almost drown trying not to laugh underwater. The minute I come up, I'm immediately looking around for that punk because I'm going to try and hold him under. Except I don't see him.

Nate's laughing from the side of the pool, looking down as I wipe my face, trying to tread water.

"Hold your breath," he yells just before I'm jerked underwater.

Oh. My. God.

I blink open to TJ's matching grin. His hair is lifted off his head, like mine. Our arms wave under the water to keep us down. Bubbles effervesce around us as he pulls my body closer to his and presses his lips to mine.

It's so cute and romantic, and it's making those drunk butterflies in my stomach twirl around all giddy. Exactly like we're doing as he holds me in one arm.

We come up together, breaching the surface just as Nate jumps in and cannonballs us.

TJ and I splash at him before he swims to go get Freddie, dragging him back to me. I hoist myself up with the help of TJ's hand on my ass, flopping back into the safety of my pink flamingo, and bask in the sun again, my guys holding on to either side, just floating with me.

"I can't believe we only have three more days. Only two nights." I breathe out, adding, "That's crazy, right?"

Three days. Eleanor's right. I'm regretting missing out on those two extra ones when we got here.

"Time flew by too fast," TJ mumbles because his chin is rested on his forearm.

I giggle at my thought. "You guys should get a house here. That way, I could talk you into letting me use it as my permanent vacation home. It could come with perks...if you know what I mean?"

Oh god, did I just say that? It's one of those things that's obviously a joke, but the truthful intent is still making me overthink.

"Damn," TJ half laughs. "The dick's that good, huh? She's all ready to move in with us, Nate."

I laugh awkwardly. "Shut up. Now that I think about it, I'd rather convince Crew and Eleanor. Less of a chance I'd have to see random chicks coming and going."

Did that make me sound jealous? Because the visual sure as hell made me feel it.

I'm so fucked.

Nate frowns, staring up at me. "Speaking of random chicks, Chads' just arrived."

TJ plays with my fingers as I lie back, pretending to close my eyes while we secretly watch Moonbeam accept the to-go boxes. Which is weird because why not just order room service. Either way, it was a stroke of genius on TJ's end once he saw their order on the bar to sabotage it.

She looks down at the one we planted a whole-ass dead fish inside, weighing it in her hands before deciding it's fine and stacking it on top of the other.

TJ chuckles. "Twenty bucks says Chad screams like a little girl and tosses it off the balcony."

Nate shakes his head. "No. He'll come down in full Karen mode, robe and all. And then we'll get to throw him in."

My smile pokes out as I say, "I bet he sends Moonbeam." My voice is mocking. "Little baby'll need his mommy to fix it."

The boys laugh, and I smile as we watch Moonbeam disappear into the hotel, and we fall back into relaxation mode. Waiting.

"Do you feel like you have closure?" TJ questions out of nowhere, making me lift my head to look at him.

"Closure? I don't need closure. I'm closed." I laugh. "You guys know this. The closest interaction I ever plan on having with Chad again is calling to cancel the rest of his dinner reservations tonight."

Nate looks over to TJ for a long moment, some kind of Tweedle exchange happening between them before Nate lifts a finger to my leg, connecting the droplets of water.

"No, you're right. You said that before. But I think we were wondering—" He clears his throat again and kind of shrugs. "—as your friends...we were just wondering if all this was helping you want to maybe get back on the market?"

As my friends? I could scream. Oh, I couldn't be worse at interpreting men. I know there's an attraction between us, clearly. And I'm also painfully aware that I'm starting to like them too much. But this...gah, is it a hint? Like, they're wondering for themselves. Or do they feel bad for me because they think I'll be back in pajamas after this with more cheesesteak stains on the front?

Why is this so hard? I feel dumb.

Dumb like the girl on *Miss Congeniality* who answered April 25th when asked to describe her perfect date.

I'm also scared, straight down to my core, over how much I want them to be asking for themselves.

Leave it to me to find myself with not one but two crushes on my fake throuple boyfriends.

What do I say? just keeps repeating itself over and over until I finally answer, hoping by the grace of anyone, really, that I don't put my foot in my mouth.

"I mean...boys, gross. Eww. It's fake relationships for life. Maybe I'll add tag teams to my Hinge profile."

Go fuck yourself, Millie. Here I am hoping not to put my foot in my mouth, and I just ate my fucking ankle.

I don't miss the way Nate looks at TJ before he dunks under the water and comes back up, saying, "I'm gonna go get some water. You want anything, Millie?"

Millie? Not Scrappy or baby. He might as well be calling me Miss Dwyer. I fucked up. I can feel it. *Why did I say that?*

As soon as they're far enough away, I paddle Freddie and me over to the opposite side of the pool, where Eleanor is lying on her lounge chair. My biceps are burning.

"Elsinore. We've got a code blue happening."

She jerks her sunglasses down, propping up on her elbows. "Who's dying?"

"My chances."

She stares at me before looking past me to where the boys are.

"Your place or mine?"

I'm already flipping off Freddie, saying, "Yours," before I hear her tell Crew to keep the guys busy because girl time is needed.

"Got it, boss," he answers, not moving a muscle.

She grabs her stuff, handing me mine as I pull out my phone.

shit you can only say in the dark

Me: Running away with Elle. See ya later.

"Jesus Christ. This room is huge. It's like an apartment, Elle." I'm turning in a circle, my eyes popping out of my head as I tuck my errant towel around my chest again. "I should've said yes when you said we could stay with you two."

She laughs, tossing her stuff on the couch and putting her hand on the back of it as she stares at me.

"Well, if you would've come up when I offered instead of getting railed nonstop, you wouldn't be filled with regret. Speaking of...what the fuck is going on? Because the whole secret agent, 'we can't say anything out loud until we got here' thing is killing me. Spill, bitch."

Oh god. I'm going to have to tell her...everything. Come totally clean. I know my face is all scrunched, giving away that I'm about to drop a secret, because she's leaning in, her eyes growing bigger and bigger.

"Millie."

I suck in a breath between my teeth before I squeeze my eyes closed and blurt it out.

"We're faking it."

My eyes pop open as she snaps, "What?"

I walk toward her, looking around for something to sit on because my bathing suit is still damp, as is the towel around me, but she repeats herself. "Millie…what?"

What is with everyone and the no nicknames today?

A whoosh of breath leaves me as I decide *fuck it*. Rich rooms probably have shit on the couches to protect them. And frankly, they can afford to replace it if I leave a permanent ass mark. So I sit, hands on my knees, as I spill it all.

"Me, TJ, and Nate…we've been faking our *situation-ship*…to get revenge on Chad. You know, since he fucked us over with the room. And after that text calling me a cleat chaser"—I'd sent a screenshot it to her the day it happened—"TJ thought up this plan. The fucking came after…the crush too. And now—"

She holds up her hand, cutting me off. Her mouth opens, then closes before her head draws back.

"Wait. What?"

This time, her voice isn't surprised or shocked. It's giddy, as if she's found out the juiciest piece of information of all time.

I'm nodding. That's all I got…just nodding. A lot.

Eleanor shakes her head. "I knew it. And you knew I knew it." She laughs. "So, when was the first time? The real time you guys…"

I clear my throat. "After our spa day. Well, it started at the spa…they kind of each cornered me, and then, you know…we came together, so to speak."

A bigger burst of laughter explodes, but she stops it in its tracks, pressing her lips together.

"Hold, please. They fucked with you *alone*...then together?"

"Yeah. Why? Is that like some kind of universal signal I don't know about?"

Eleanor heads straight to the minibar...which is like a whole-ass regular bar. *Damn.* She grabs a bottle of Patrón before making her way back to the couch and plops down, folding her legs in crisscross with a giant grin on her face.

"Yeah, now we know they like-like you. Just trust me...I'm your complicated-situations bible right now."

I roll my eyes, chuckling. "Okay, fine. But even if that's true, I told them this was for the week, or they may have never agreed in the first place. That was the understanding. We expire. I can't just change it up now. And frankly, the odds of a miracle don't seem in my favor. Not even with your help, sexual Jesus."

"Oh, ye of little faith..." She arranges the shot glasses and pours, laughing at her own joke. "The answer is so fucking obvious."

I let out a drawn-out exhale, but she raises her glass, driving home her point.

"You need to give them a preview. Boys are love-stupid, Mills. Delicious and funny. Amazing to have around. But they need things spelled out for them. Just take the Tweedles on an actual date. No revenge. No me and Crew. Just you guys out in the world, throupling it up. Show them what they could have. Because given the choice...nobody turns you down."

She clinks her glass to mine. "It's bad bitch o'clock."

I smile and shoot back the damn liquor before I say, "Love you the most."

"Duh." She winks. "We're soulmates. Now, let's strategize the setting. Because you're keeping your dicks."

twenty-five

. . .

"Awww, look who's simpin' for the girl."

tweedles

tj

> QB1: Your girl's in my room too sleepy to function. And I can't bring her to you because I've got my hands full with her dumbass friend...my fiancé.

I look up at Nate, shoving my dinner away. "We gotta go get Smalls."

He laughs, getting up off the chair. "All right. Let me get my shoes."

> Me: Tell her we're on our way.

When she bailed on us today, I knew it was because of our questions.

Nate was trying to feel her out, and I was following

205

his lead. But it was the dumbest thing we could do. Actually, no. Breaking all our rules and starting to fall for the one emotionally unavailable girl around is the dumbest.

Fuck me. I swear to god, I was nervous today, looking up at her in that pool. I've never wanted a girl to like me back so much.

The big dummy sliding on his sneakers feels the same too. After she left, for the rest of the afternoon, we were quiet, letting Crew do most of the talking.

Because I don't know about Nate, but it wasn't as fun without her. She didn't even get to see Chad rush out onto his balcony screaming as he chucked a dead fish off the side of it.

"You ready?" he grumbles, and I nod.

But when I stand up, I stretch my arms.

"Dude, it feels like she's the one that's getting away. *The one*…ya know? I'm telling you, she'll be the thing that makes us like the DiCaprios of the world."

His shoulders shake. "So we'll start tag teaming supermodels. We already do that."

"No, you asshole. We'll be out-of-shape jerk-offs because we let go of Kate Winslet's hand and drown."

He rubs a hand down his jaw. "Did you actually watch the movie? Cuz none of what you said makes sense. She let him go."

I smirk, scratching my neck. "Oh. Nah, I fell asleep. That shit was too long."

He laughs and shoves my shoulder. "Regardless, I fucking get it. But let's just bring her back because not having her around sucked today."

I follow Nate out of the room, teasing him, "Awww, look who's simpin' for the girl."

"Shut the fuck up, or I'll hit you so hard you'll swallow your own tongue."

We laugh and joke the whole way to Crew's, heading to get our little drunk buddy and bring her back to tuck her in.

It takes us all of five minutes to walk to the nicer side of the hotel. The one that has the minibars and infinity pools and butlers.

Damn. Fuck Chad. Forever.

The moment we arrive, I spy the door open. Crew hooked it up for us. I push it open, Nate trailing behind as we walk in.

My eyes immediately land on Mills. She's cuddled in an oversized chair, her head resting on the back and fuzzy blanket around her.

Damn. She's too fucking cute for words.

Crew jerks his chin in greeting, not speaking as he bends down to scoop Eleanor up into his arms. She mumbles something, but he just smiles and answers, "Once everyone's gone, wild card."

Nate closes the distance to Mills, running the backs of his knuckles over her cheeks. "Millie. Baby. You wanna walk, or you want me to carry you?"

She sighs, not opening her eyes or speaking. Instead, she lifts her arms above her head with a soft, dreamy smile on her face.

He smiles before he reaches down, grabbing her ass with both hands and scooping her up. She wraps around him like a little koala, nuzzling her face into the side of his neck.

He turns toward me as I grab her shoes and bag. I jog ahead, opening our door and letting them go first before I quietly close it behind me.

She sleeps the whole way, cuddling closer to Nate occasionally. Her arms are locked around his neck, and his hand gently strokes her back, the other still holding her up.

The thing about this is that him holding her doesn't bother me. At all.

I'm not jealous. I'm happy she's comfortable and sleeping.

This is nothing that I've ever felt before. I like seeing him take care of what's ours. Oh fuck. *Ours*. She could be that. The one who changes us.

Damn, that's the kind of thought that takes the wind right out of a guy.

We stop at the door, and I use my key to open it. She doesn't let go of him until he walks into the bedroom and lays her down gently.

I set her stuff on the dresser before sitting next to her, brushing her hair out of her face.

"You wanna sleep in your bathing suit? Or you want to take it off?"

Her quiet, raspy voice makes me melt.

"No. Naked. It's hot."

Nate unties her top, taking it off as I busy myself with the bottoms, freeing her. We toss them on the floor as she extends her arms, reaching in either direction to the sides of the bed.

"In." She's opening and closing her hands, calling for us to come into bed with her. "I want you."

We look at each other and silently laugh. Because she's definitely drunk. We drag our clothes off with zero intentions of fucking this girl, because that's not what she needs right now, before sliding in and positioning her between us.

Nate guides one of her legs over his hip as her palms rest on his chest, and I sink down behind her, snaking my arm up her chest so my palm outstretches over her clavicle.

Holding her tight to me.

She sighs a little happy hum, and I feel her body relax as her sleepy voice fills the space.

"We should stay like this forever."

Don't we wish.

twenty-six

. . .

"You're like Lara Croft but hotter."

millie

The minute I woke up, I had to hit the ground running.

After my session with love doctor Eleanor, we not only worked up my nerves for today, but we got all the shit together for it too.

"Thanks again for getting this picnic basket ready at the last minute. You don't know how much this means to me."

The clerk who witnessed my check-in from hell smiles back at me.

"It was my pleasure, especially after your introduction to our hotel. And by the way, you can call me Paul."

I smile. "You know, Paul, it's actually been a pretty amazing trip."

He leans forward conspiratorially. "Well, just so you know, we like to look out for our favorite clientele… That being said, Mr. Ajax never seems to get his room

210

service to his room before it's ice-cold, and suspiciously hasn't been able to get a new towel during his entire stay."

I laugh, my jaw dropping.

"Okay...I'm not calling you Paul—I'm calling you my bestie. You're freaking amazing, and that is definitely by far elite-level service. Sir, I will make sure to leave a five-star review on every available site."

He smiles and winks before his eyes brighten, and he snaps his fingers.

"I almost forgot. Your costumes for the party arrived. They were very fast. Apparently, nobody ever wants to use them. So you lucked out."

"Really?" I ponder, completely dumbfounded. "That baffles me. Yay me, I guess."

My idea for the *Lovers Only* rager the hotel is throwing may go down as best costume ever.

And the fact that there's a $5,000 prize for best costume is icing on the cake. Because the guys and I are a lock.

I slide the basket off the counter. "Will you have them delivered to our room?"

He nods, saying, "Of course," before I tap the counter and turn to head out to the Jeep I've rented.

There's definitely a pep in my step. I can't help it.

It's not every day a girl gets to wine and dine two boys at the same time. I feel like the Bachelorette.

Except I don't get a fantasy suite. I do get railed though, so who's really winning?

I'm holding the basket with both hands, swinging it slightly as I walk. My knees gently bounce off it before I set it to the ground in front of the Jeep, then pat my back pockets, looking for my phone.

I smile to myself because they're going to be so excited.

Time to get Operation Tweedles in order.

> Me: Get your trunks and towels. We have plans. Lobby in ten, boys.

> TJ: Yes ma'am

> Nate: You got it, baby.

"WHERE ARE WE GOING?" TJ CHUCKLES, DUCKING UNDER A big palm as Nate smacks his arm, probably bitten by a mosquito.

In theory, this seemed like an amazing idea. Find the elusive waterfall that TJ had us on a wild-goose chase for the other day. Spend the day together, maybe get it on.

Basically, heaven.

Although, in application, this is looking like a fail.

We might be lost in the jungle.

I blame all early 2000 rom-coms because they've ruined my perspective on life, really making me seek out a damn moment.

This was supposed to be my montage. The thing that would play back in their heads before we said goodbye.

"Hmm," I say to myself, trying not to laugh at the stupidity in my brain. Looking down at my phone again to read the directions, I whisper, "Under the largest palm tree by the giant rock with the white spot."

I should have known better than to listen to the room service guy who brought me and Eleanor pizza last night in all our tipsy-girl glory. We started hounding him about waterfalls because we'd just come up with this idea.

He's sent me here to die because I was annoying.

I look around, searching for either a palm tree or a polka-dot rock, when TJ and Nate grab my waist and chin respectively, forcing me to shuffle to my left until my gaze finally locks on exactly what I'm looking for.

"Yes," I shout, bouncing up and down excitedly, pointing to the rock. "We're here."

TJ looks at Nate, who laughs. "This is awesome, Mills. Really tropical. What is this exactly?"

I laugh because they're looking at me like I've lost it, so I shove his shoulder. "No, silly. Follow me."

They do, holding the towels and basket as I cut through some more trees before finally coming to the clearing of all clearings.

I spin around to face them, my arms outstretched as I say, "Ta-daaaa."

Awe is written all over their faces. It's perfect. Exactly the reaction I was hoping for. I spin to take it in too.

The eighty-foot waterfall is something to be seen. Water mists around us as it crashes into the pool below. There's even a rainbow shimmering in it.

"It's so beautiful," I whisper. "Not gonna lie, for a minute there, I was worried we weren't going to find it, making us o for two."

"You're like Lara Croft but hotter," Nates chuckles, coming to stand beside me.

TJ lets out a long whistle from behind me. "Holy shit, Smalls. This is fucking insane. I can't believe you found it."

"Yeah." I smile, turning around and putting my hands on TJ's waist, looking up at him. "I wanted today to be special. Just us. A way to say thank you." I look over at Nate, who's already smiling down at me. "You guys turned this whole week around. I owed you one."

TJ leans down, kissing the side of my head before I'm pulled into Nate's arms, and he kisses me too.

"Hey," Nate says with a wink. "You wanna be bad?"

I nod my head slowly, hearing TJ's half laugh.

Nate leans in closer, kissing my lips gently. "I'm thinking we don't really need swim trunks." His finger hooks around the bikini string tied around my neck. "And you don't need this pesky little thing either."

I bite my bottom lip, giving an innocent shrug.

"I mean...I guess you're right. We *are* secluded."

TJ's fingers tickle my neck as he begins untying it. I try and hide my grin, but it's no use because my top glides off, completely freed seconds later.

The faintest smirk blooms on the side of Nate's face as he looks over at TJ again and shrugs. "Whoops."

I laugh as the boys strip before running off the small cliff we're on and jumping directly down into the water, coming up howling.

"Fuck, it's cold," Nate thunders, shaking his head, making his hair whip sideways.

TJ waves me in. "Get in here and keep us warm."

Oh shit. I hope this moment stays forever ingrained like some callback to wild days and hopefully wild nights.

I let out a breath and run before, for the very first time, I really let myself fall. But that thought's only romantic for about thirty-two seconds until I hit the water, and then a scream that starts from under the water bleeds to on top.

"*Cold.*"

The boys are hysterically laughing, yelling for me to "get over here" as they swim toward me.

I squeal, swimming backward, but it's no use because they catch up too quickly.

I'm breathless and swooning, pulled into Nate's arms, my bare breasts against his chest. He holds both of us above the water. His wet lips touch mine, pressing awkwardly as he treads water for the both of us.

"Hold on," he breathes before shifting me onto his back, my arms wrapped around his neck.

The three of us swim through the pond, and I look around at the banks of tropical trees, birds flying sporadically.

Wow. Nothing will ever beat this moment.

Nate's shoulders tense, so I hold on tighter as the pounding of water gets louder. TJ looks over at me, his hazel eyes so bright, a smile on his face.

"Under," he shouts, and I nod just before Nate ducks both of us under the water. TJ follows suit, going underneath the cascade.

We pop up within seconds of each other behind the falls. It's dank and a little dark, but there are rocks stacked up, making it shallow enough to sit in the hidden enclosure.

I didn't even do any of the work, but I'm still breathing kind of heavy. Or maybe it's because we're in a makeshift cave that I can hear it better.

Either way, the chorus of quiet, slow panting between the three of us is making it feel like we're already doing something we shouldn't.

"This is cool," I say, letting go of Nate just before TJ reaches for my hand, his eyes ticking to my tits, then back.

He helps me up on the rock bench as I look over my shoulder through the water before I sit.

Nobody could see us unless they were really looking.

My legs dangle in the water as I'm sandwiched between the two of them, my head shifting back and forth. They haven't spoken.

They're just looking at me. I swear the magnitude of that, both their eyes on me, shakes me to the core. It's overwhelming. Especially since I'm pretty sure I know what they're thinking.

Everything is quieter behind the falls. Like we're vacuum sealed in here. Except our intentions are starting to scream.

I lick my lips, staring down at the water as I give in to the voice in my head and graze my fingers over their thighs.

Deep inhales come from either side, making me grin again as I touch them. I glide up and down, just a bit higher each time.

TJ slicks his hair back as Nate wipes his own hand down his face.

"You're cold," TJ breathes with a smirk.

I shake my head because I feel fine, but he reaches up, caressing one of my breasts, lazily rubbing his thumb over my pebbled nipple.

It makes *me* shiver, and his smirk turns into a smile.

Nate's Adam's apple bobs as he swallows, watching what TJ's doing to me before he licks some water from his lips.

"Ah," I let out quietly, almost as a sigh, feeling Nate's lips touch my shoulder gently. My eyes drift close as his hand slides over my stomach and back.

"Your body is so beautiful," Nate whispers before his hand stops by my hip.

TJ's gently pinching my other nipple now, rolling it between his fingers, manipulating every goddamn nerve ending present. Nate's fingertip runs over a scar that I got falling off my bicycle when I was ten.

"I like this," he breathes, feeling the raised scar and kissing my shoulder again. "I always feel it when I'm holding your hips, and it makes me wanna know…"

His voice trails off, not finishing the sentence, even though he still strokes the spot.

My lashes flutter open because TJ pinches just hard enough to make even the parts of me in the water begin to warm.

I suck in a quiet breath between my teeth, but he sticks out his bottom lip like he's pouting.

"Did it hurt? Lemme kiss it better."

TJ's eyes gently caress my body before he reaches down, taking my hand off his thigh and running the backs of my knuckles up his hard abs, further up his chest, until he pulls it away and brings the inside of my wrist to his lips.

"That's not what you pinched," Nate whispers, drawing my eyes to his.

They're crinkled a little at the sides as they drop to my lips.

"I know," TJ answers before leaning down, licking my nipple, and drawing it between his lips.

My lips part as an exhale escapes. That's all the invitation Nate needs because he leans in, sealing his mouth to mine.

It's not his usual kiss, domineering and rough. This

one's slow. Every movement of his lips feels like he's savoring me. Nate's bottom lip glides in between mine before we tilt our heads, letting our tongues taste and tease.

They barely touch, drawing back before diving in again as TJ matches the rhythm over my nipple.

Their lips are so fucking soft and warm.

I could do this for hours and feel satisfied.

Nate cradles my face, his fingers woven into my hair. They pull at the strands as he tugs me a bit closer, the kiss growing deeper.

He growls into my mouth, pulling me closer again, away from TJ.

My hands lock around Nate's wrist and neck as TJ's hands stroke my back.

"Fuck, you're beautiful," TJ rushes out, tracing his palm down my spine.

But I can barely concentrate. Nate's mouth is hungry. It's possessing me, becoming more fevered. I moan against his lips, moving my hands to his chest.

That's when the Nate I know shows up, rough and wanting, but before he can take what he wants, I feel TJ's hands slip under my chin and drag me away.

"My turn," he growls.

But that doesn't stop Nate because he just keeps kissing over my cheek, then toward my neck, as I'm ripped away and TJ's mouth takes its place.

His tongue dives inside, swirling with mine as Nate sucks on my neck.

"I want you marked," Nate groans as if the idea makes him hard.

My body's turned toward TJ now, forcing Nate to lift my hair before I feel his lips seal to the back of my neck. I tangle my fingers into TJ's hair as he hums appreciatively, kissing me with the kind of passion two people share when they're driven by need.

It's sloppy and desperate. Our mouths are fucking.

His hands come to both sides of my head, holding me in place as he kisses the fuck out of me as if he can barely contain himself.

The sounds of our lust mix with the water gently lapping around us.

"Mmmm," I moan as Nate moves to another spot, leaving another hickey on my body.

My thighs squeeze together, one knee drawing up, already craving friction.

Nate's palm snakes around the front of my body, cupping my breast as he says, "My turn again."

This time, I'm not turned away from TJ, but our mouths still disconnect as I'm pressed backward by Nate, laid over both their laps.

My chest's rising and falling because I'm fucking breathless. TJ's kissed it all out of me.

I run my hands over my own body, watching them look at me. All of me.

Fucking me with their eyes. I'm starting to think I'll never not want it.

I stare straight up into Nate's eyes as TJ pushes my bikini bottom to the side crudely as if he's entitled, exposing my sex as he swipes a finger over my slit only to bring it to his mouth and taste.

"I love how wet your pussy gets, Smalls," TJ offers with a smirk.

Fuck. Me. I can feel the ends of my hair dragging with the motion of the water as I try and catch my breath, but it's no use because they do this to me.

Nate's hand rubs up and down my stomach before he

cups one of my tits and leans down, kissing it. He kisses my flesh, running his tongue over my entire areola before licking the hard bud.

I gasp, sucking in air and arching my back, pressing my tits closer to his face as my legs part. TJ slides his hand back under my bikini bottoms, ghosting his fingers over my clit, making me shiver and cry out before he dives between my pussy.

"Oh god. Yes. Fuck me like that."

"Baby," Nate growls, urging me to twist sideways as he jerks his cock. "You talking like that makes me want to do filthy shit to you."

My pussy gushes because I want him in my mouth. His hard cock is against his stomach, so I lean closer, flattening my tongue and licking up the underside of his shaft.

"Goddamn, you just got so fucking wet," TJ groans, spreading my arousal around my pussy before he thrusts two fingers inside me. "Ask me why there's two fingers, Millie."

I'm using Nate's thigh to prop myself up halfway as I turn my head to look at TJ's face.

"Why?" I say breathlessly.

He thrusts them inside again, rubbing his thumb over my clit, making me shudder and my eyes almost roll back.

"One for me." He draws them out slowly. "And one for Nate." They're pushed inside again as he grins. "Because my dirty bitch only likes it in pairs."

Fuck. I'm arrested by need. So I turn my face and suck the head of Nate's cock into my mouth, wanting him to fuck my face while TJ finger fucks me.

"Millie," Nate groans, gripping my hair. "Easy, baby.

Fuck. That's so good."

But I don't go easy. I make it my business to suck his cock, hollowing my cheeks as I bob my head.

TJ's fingers glide in and out of my pussy, rubbing my clit, pressing over the swollen mound, creating the perfect amount of friction.

My hips rock, meeting every pound of TJ's fingers, and I suck and suck, moaning around Nate's shaft, running my tongue around the rim, letting him almost pull out before deep-throating him.

Nate's words are stuttered, like he's holding his breath in between them as he cradles my jaw.

"I think we created a monster."

TJ chuckles, finger fucking me faster, making my body buck. "Whores suck cock. And ours loves cum down her throat, don't you, slut?"

Fuck. I didn't think my pussy could get any wetter, but it does.

Nate breathes harshly through his nose before his grip tightens. "Those lips look beautiful stretched around my cock. You were meant to suck my dick, baby."

I can feel his hips begin to grind, forcing his cock deeper toward the back of my throat.

"That's it. Suck his cock." TJ exhales roughly. "Let him use you while I lick up the mess."

No sooner does TJ say that than he slips down between my legs and flattens his tongue and slowly licks my pussy like a fucking ice cream cone.

The moan that rips from my chest vibrates around Nate's dick. And it's music to his ears because he rolls his hips, lifting himself up with a palm on the rocks to angle himself better.

And he fucks my face.

I'm held in place as he hits the back of my throat over and over. I gag, eyes watering, trying to suck and keep up with his pace, but my head is spinning because TJ is devouring my pussy.

The build starts to roll over and over in my body, building higher and higher.

TJ's licking and sucking on my clit before he leaves it, only to spit on my cunt and eat again. It's degrading and fucking delicious.

"You want me to make this pussy cry, baby," he growls against my clit.

Fuck. I want it. I want to come.

His fingers join, pushing in and out, sliding between my lips to spread me wider so he can flick my clit with his tongue before he sucks again. I shiver, trying to open my legs wider for him to lick me more.

Nate's eyes are on mine as he fucks my face without mercy as his words rain down.

"Suck that cock, baby. And keep your fucking eyes on me. I want to watch the way you look when I come down that pretty throat."

Oh my god. I'm whimpering, fingernails digging into the rock as my other hand searches for TJ's head, curling my fingers into his hair. I need it—him eating my pussy more and more.

My hips rock faster, circling too, begging for him to make me come. He hums, attacking my pussy, making my stomach contract.

"Come on my face," TJ groans, diving back to lick me, letting the sound echo off the stone walls. "Let me swallow your cum while you swallow his."

"Fuck," Nate growls, thrown over the edge by the same vision I got. "I'm gonna come."

I'm staring at Nate like he told me to as TJ buries his face between my legs relentlessly.

Nate grinds harder and faster, grunting, pulling the strands of my hair violently hard as his jaw tenses. He's chasing his release as my eyelashes flutter, my own beginning to take over.

"Yes, baby. Yes, baby. Make me come..." His voice is barely spoken above the tension his whole body locks into. "I'm gonna come down that fucking throat until I'm the only thing you'll ever taste."

Warm, salty spurts hit the roof of my mouth as he sucks in a harsh breath.

And that's all I needed.

My body explodes, coating TJ's mouth with cum. I'm moaning, but it's muffled as Nate drips down my throat. TJ growls, his palm coming to my stomach, anchoring my lifted body in place as he licks all the most sensitive parts of me clean.

He doesn't stop. His tongue laves over my sex as if he can't get enough.

I swallow, and Nate slowly pulls his cock out of my mouth, wiping his thumb over my lips.

"So pretty all used up," he whispers down at me as I pant.

TJ licks over my clit again, making me quiver because I'm too sensitive, before he looks ups and growls, "Me."

TJ reaches for me, pulling me onto his lap and directly onto his cock. I suck in a deep breath. His cock is so big that it never gets easier.

And I like that.

He makes it hurt in the best way.

I ride him slow, my hands on his shoulders as he

watches me, reaching between my legs to spread my pussy, looking at his cock slide in and out of me.

My hips rock forward as I fuck him, his hands tightening on my hips.

"Millie," he moans, "I want to fuck you. Like a fucking animal. And I wanna come on your back so that you're mine. Let me make you mine."

Oh fuck. How does he always hit every fucking nerve with that mouth?

"Yes. Make me yours."

TJ lifts me off him, repositioning me so that I'm standing on a lower rock with my ass in front of him. Nate takes my hands, placing them on his chest like a human wall for me to hold on to as TJ circles the head of his cock at my entrance, his forehead against my back before he hammers back inside me.

The moment his cock bottoms out inside my pussy, he doesn't slow down. TJ fucks me hard, forcing me to hold on to Nate, whose eyes are locked on mine.

My entire body bucks over and over as TJ shows no mercy. I'm blinking too fast, my mouth fallen open.

Nate slaps his hands over mine as they start to slip.

"Take that cock like a good girl," Nate coaxes. "Let that pussy get fucked. He'll ruin it. You'll be fucking ruined for anyone else."

I'm whimpering as TJ wraps an arm around my waist, bringing our bodies flush, filth falling from his mouth. "Squeeze that fucking cunt around my cock. That's it. This is my pussy."

Nate growls, not letting go of my eyes. "Is this his pussy, Millie? Or mine? You fucking answer me, slut."

Nate lets go of one of my hands, dipping down to my clit, and rubs. "Right now. Tell him who this belongs to."

I can't speak. My body is overloaded. I'm not just building again—I'm coming.

"Millie," TJ bellows, fucking me harder and harder, rutting into me. "You fucking tell *him* this is mine, or I'll starve it to death. You'll never come again."

White, blinding light is blurring my vision, and my eyes roll back into my head because I'm gone. So orgasmic that I'm in a different fucking consciousness.

Whatever else they say, I don't hear because the scream coming out of my mouth is the only sound filling the space.

I jerk, held by both of them as TJ stills, coming all over me. I can barely breathe as I open my eyes to Nate's smile. We're still for a moment, calming until I look over my shoulder, watching TJ milk his cock.

White ropes of cum drip over my back and ass as he grins down. "Mine," he says breathlessly. "Fucking mine."

"Yours," I answer, drawing his eyes before I turn back to Nate. "And yours." I inhale a slow breath, letting it out before I add, "Because this dirty bitch likes her cock in pairs too."

Nate laughs, leaning in and kissing me softly, whispering, "Good girl."

And damn if I don't want to say, "No, *your* girl," back to him.

twenty-seven

. . .

"Not in the year of Harry Styles and his jumpsuit gyration."

millie

We're still laughing as Nate pulls into the valet. The whole day's been perfect. Incredible, actually. We swam, fucked, swam, ate, and then I got eaten again.

The only hiccup was when two older women stumbled upon our blue lagoon. I would've apologized for our nudity, but my mouth was full of TJ. So...that wasn't exactly ideal, but at least we cleared out of there quickly. Especially when they said they were calling the police.

I swear Nate pulled out from where we were parked on the side of the road so fast he's now an honorary *Fast & Furious* cast member. I can smell burnt rubber.

I scoot forward in the back seat, my hands on their seats. "You don't think anyone got our plate number, do you?"

TJ shakes his head, unbuckling before he gets out.

"Nah, and they couldn't prove it was us anyway. Those women were too far away to pick us out of a lineup."

"So, why'd we run, then?"

"Just in case," Nate levels before coming around the front of the Jeep, winking at me. "One good photo and we end up unemployed. I'm not so sure the NFL would be stoked over a public indecency arrest."

The guys are laughing, but I shake my head. I can just imagine their contract negotiations.

Please add a sex-in-public clause because these deviants can't keep it in their pants.

We're walking into the lobby, teasing each other and laughing, my hand in TJ's as I hold Nate's waistband. And a thought strikes me hard.

I'm going to tell them how I feel as soon we get to the room.

"Hey," TJ tosses out, "are you ever going to tell us what we're going as for the Lovers thing?"

I shake my head. "No. It's a surprise."

Nate's chuckling, about to pester me too just as Paul waves, calling my name. "Miss Dwyer." He's all smiles, looking like my favorite dapper villain as he makes his way around the counter and greets the boys.

"Gentlemen. I'm glad I caught you."

"Oh, Paul." I snap my fingers. "Shoot, I left the basket in the Jeep. Let me go and grab it really quick."

He protests politely, "Miss Dwyer, we can handle it. You don't need to do that."

But I wave him off. "No, it's fine."

To be honest, I'd brought condoms with us just in case anyone wanted to double-dip, so I need to get those out before people wonder why I have enough condoms for an orgy.

Thankfully, the car is still in its spot, so I trot over and look inside, seeing the basket as far out of my reach as possible.

"Great," I whisper to myself, climbing in and grabbing it before awkwardly snagging my loot back and shoving it into my back pockets. I'm slinking backward out of the car, trying not to ding the basket, as I hear my name from behind me.

"Millie."

My forehead wrinkles, partially because the voice is familiar. And partially because I'm instantly irritated.

My hair swishes over my shoulder as I turn and lock eyes with Chad.

Fucking *Chad*.

"I'd almost forgotten you were still here."

He winces because he was expertly hit. *Guess whose sharp-ass tongue is working now, Chad…mine.*

"Well, here I am." He shrugs, walking closer. "And I'm happy to see you."

I narrow my eyes, motioning to the valet area. "Were you thinking of taking a jog into traffic? Don't let me keep you."

He reaches for my elbow, but I smack his hand away, glancing over his shoulder to try and spot the guys. But I don't see them. Until I do, stalking my way. *Shit.*

"Jesus, Millie," he rushes out. "I just want to talk to you."

"Then use your fucking mouth and not your hands, Chad."

But as I spit my words out, I pull my phone out of my pocket, condoms spilling out as I type quickly in our group chat, trying to decompress the situation.

> **Me:** I'm good. I'll catch up with you guys later.

They freeze, pulling out their phones and reading the message before looking at each other and then at me, jaws tensed but bodies moving backward.

I got this, guys. It's about time I solidified some closure and used my own fucking voice.

Chad takes a deep breath, running his hands through his hair. "Listen, there's a lot to say. And I have to be honest…" He shoves his hands into his front pockets, looking down before he glances up, forehead wrinkled. "I haven't stopped thinking about you since the day you got here."

Oh my god. I can't believe I fell for this shit once.

"What in the One Direction?" I whisper to myself.

He's trying to boy band me. He's doing the cheeseball swoony look an autotuned lead singer gives into a camera before he says something like, *"Girl. You know it's always been you."*

Gross. Not in the year of Harry Styles and his jump-suit gyration.

"Funny," I scoff. "And here I thought Moonbeam was your focus… you remember your girlfriend, right?"

He smirks, and I want to dry heave as he says, "I'm glad to see she affects you."

I have a physical reaction. My whole body shakes as I lift my hands into fists before spitting, "Ohh, don't flatter yourself. I don't give a fuck who you do or don't date. If you haven't noticed, I myself have been *very* busy."

He looks over his shoulder, smirking slimily as he turns back.

"I know, baby—"

229

Baby? What the fuck? His voice is weirdly low, like he's trying to sound like he owns a pair.

Chad steps in even closer, this time reaching for my waist. *Noooooo.*

I shove his hand away, putting the basket between us, but he brings it back like he's reading something I'm definitely not throwing out.

"Trust me, Mills. I've noticed, and if you want me to admit that I'm jealous, I will—"

I slap at his hands, my head drawing further back, horror marring my face as I shake my head.

"—because we've got two days left here, and we could salvage our trip. We could be together." He sighs dramatically, trying to cradle my face, but I wiggle it"I know you loved me. Your boyfriends spilled the beans. And I think I love you too…"

Oh my god. I'll kill them.

"Noooo. Unhuhh… Hard pass," I draw out, realizing what's about to happen.

But it's too late. I'm fucking assaulted, straight up hurled into trauma because Chad locks his thin, chapped lips on mine.

The sound that leaves my body can only be compared to those shrieking goats because that's the only way I can say, "Ewwwwwww," with my fucking mouth closed.

I stand there frozen, my stupid body deciding on that instead of flight, even though my mind is chanting, *Run, bitch, run for your fucking life.*

For fuck's sake, he's like a fucking demon trying to suck the life out of me. There's no shot I'll ever open my mouth. I'd rather pull every muscle in my face than let that happen.

Finally, my mind and body catch up and join forces. I

drop the basket before my hands weave into his hair, and I pull it. Really fucking hard.

"Oww," he whines before I smack against his puny chest with all the disgust I own and push him away.

I shiver, wildly icked out, as Chad stumbles back with unjustifiable surprise all over his face. He stares back at me, and it's all so fucking dramatic that I can't take it. Is this guy serious?

One of his hands actually reaches for me.

I'll chop it off. Chop, chop, chop.

"Millie," he whispers. "Don't do this."

I wipe my mouth with the back of my hand and my fingers, saying all the things I should've said long ago.

"No. Do not Millie me. Absolutely not. I'm not getting over you, Chad... I'm way fucking past you. You were never good enough for me. I think I just fucked you because you were a DJ, and it's like one of those things you scratch off your bucket list. I just forgot I wasn't supposed to fall in love with you. And looking back...I don't even think I really was. The bar was already set so low by a bevy of mediocre men like yourself that average became normal. I thought I had to settle in order to have someone. But I'm really happy that you did what you did. Because I may have never been open to the two amazing men I have now. And no offense, Ajax. I hope that Moonbeam leaves you because you should be forced to live with you, by yourself...that way, you can understand why you're so fucking unlikable."

The look on his face when I say Moonbeam's name tells me everything I need to know. I almost laugh, but instead, my mouth drops open as I stare at him.

Something tells me the only reason Chad's standing here right now is because I'm his last resort.

"Oh my god," I rush out.

But before I can say another thing, DJ Dookie breaks. Like, fully dissolves into a puddle. His face distorts into an uglier version of the Kardashian cry face as he descends upon me, arms around my neck, barely making any sense as he blubbers on my shoulder.

"She left me," he weeps, sucking in snot. "She ran off with Scottie. The fucking surf instructor…I shit my pants, Millie, and she left me for the guy who hosed me down."

My mouth hasn't closed as I blink too fast. This isn't happening.

How is this happening?

I'm frozen in place, trying to figure out what to do. "Fuck," I breathe out and just give in, wrapping my arms around him, bracing as he cries harder.

"It's okay," I say, patting his back, trying not to die of embarrassment as people look. "You're going to be good, dude."

This could and does only happen to me.

"Chad." I try and extract myself from his grip, but he pulls me back in, crying louder. *Jesus.* I wrench his arms off me, my palm smacked to his chest.

"You need to pull it together. Maybe head back to your room and wash your face. Take a breather. And stop crying in public."

"Okay," he whispers, nodding, his voice cracking. "Yeah, good idea. You always have good ideas. But maybe this all happened for a reason."

"No. Nope." I spit and spin him toward another entrance as I pat his back. "You need to walk it off."

He looks over his shoulder one more time before finally walking away. And thank god, too, because the laugh finally breaks as I pick up my mangled basket and head back inside, talking to myself. "Fucking Scottie... and way to go, Moonbeam."

I get ten feet in the door, still chuckling to myself, thinking about how the guys are going to react to this clusterfuck, when I look up and lock eyes with them.

The look on their respective faces is almost unreadable...almost, because what I can tell is that they saw Chad kiss me.

And they really didn't like it.

twenty-eight

. . .

"He's got a hot little Gemini rising who's
keeping him company."

nate

"Hey," Millie rushes out, shifting her face between us, "it's not what you think."

TJ's chin is lifted so that he's staring above her, so he tugs his shirt.

"Hey. Come on. Don't do that. It was nothing. Seriously."

I clear my throat, plucking her hand but not holding it. "You don't owe us an explanation, Millie. It's none of our business."

She scrunches her nose, looking at me for a second before dipping her shoulder and shoving her hands into her back pockets. "I know…but it's just… He kissed *me*. I almost punched him. Then he cried because apparently Moon—"

TJ cuts her off. "It's none of our business, like Nate said. It's cool though…we believe you, Mills. It's just—"

He doesn't finish, interlocking his hands behind his

neck. Probably to keep himself from touching her because that's why I just crossed my arms.

"Right," she breathes out, shrugging. "Okay, yeah. No details...sorry. Nothing like my old *real* relationship colliding with my fake one."

Damn. That was right between the eyes.

She looks uncomfortable, standing here like she doesn't know what to say, chewing the inside of her cheek.

Everything that used to feel so natural between the three of us suddenly feels awkward as fuck.

But I don't get time to focus on that.

Paul approaches again with a key packet. "Here you are, gentlemen. It may only be for two nights, but I'm sure two queen beds are better than a pullout."

I give him a nod, pocketing it. And like the consummate professional Paul is, he steps away, leaving us alone again.

"We got a new room?" she rasps, looking up at me.

I shake my head, hating myself for being such a fucking asshole. But sometimes self-preservation is all a guy has.

She's staring at me, and I see the confusion, and it royally fucking sucks.

An hour ago, she was ours.

But two seconds ago, we were reminded she isn't.

We aren't real. We expire on Sunday like two ugly, overgrown Cinderellas.

And it's not about Chad kissing her. But it fucking took *him* to wake us up.

Because that kiss was more real than anything we can give her.

We want what we can't have. Which is the ultimate

catch-fucking-22 since the only place I want to be is next to Millie.

And maybe not saying anything to her about how we feel makes both of us fucking cowards instead of respectful of her boundaries. Or maybe we're being selfish protecting ourselves from the kind of slaughter getting turned down would feel like.

All I know is that choosing two more nights with her knowing it's our last supper isn't something either of us can stomach.

It's too hard.

I need some fucking reprieve. All this "catching feelings" shit is too hard. I thought it just came with liking her, but apparently, I get to feel all the other emotions too.

"Wait a minute," she presses, her face shifting to TJ's. "Why are you guys moving into your own room?" She hitches a thumb over her shoulder, her brows drawn together. "Are you serious? Because of what just happened? I told you—"

"No," TJ breaks in, his hands coming to her face as he stares down at her. "No...we believe you. You didn't even have to explain. We'd always believe you, Mills."

Her hands cover his as she stares up at him, and it guts me for him. How is he handling this?

TJ takes a deep breath. "It's just easier this way, Smalls. You know? A cleaner break. The waterfall was... it was amazing. And you were...but..."

Millie quietly gasps, blinking quickly. "But you don't date the girls you...I get it. Yeah." She lets out a whoosh of a breath, gently removing TJ's hands. "It's cool. That makes sense. Our expiration date is almost upon us. And there's really no more revenge needed." She laughs, but it's off as she takes another step back. "No. It's a good decision."

She swallows, and I swear there's something I can't make out on her face. And that feels like it's going to haunt me.

"Millie," I level, and she smiles, but it's one I've never seen.

Because it's fake.

"No. Seriously. All good here. You guys go stretch out. And I'll finally get to sleep with a blanket since I won't be sandwiched between two space heaters."

She turns away before spinning back. "I'm actually gonna head over to Eleanor's to tell her the Chad story, so you can grab your stuff. Just leave me the extra key."

We nod, neither of us saying a fucking word as she walks away. *Shit.*

There are very few times in my life when I've instantly regretted a decision.

But this is one.

"Did we fuck up?" TJ breathes, looking at me.

So, I nod. "Yeah. We fucked up good."

millie

I don't know if they stood there and watched me go because I didn't look back. I'm done playing the fool for a shot at love.

Jesus, that sounds like a reality show.

I'm such an idiot. A stupid hopeless romantic who

never learns. Did I really think that if I took them on a date, they'd break a rule they've had in place since they started their careers in pussy?

Why did I listen to Eleanor? Why? As if I haven't known her my whole life.

Speaking of, I pull my phone back out from my pocket to text her, another fucking condom falling out, so I kick it. Sending it flying.

Right into bare feet... adorned with a million anklets.

Hold up. My face pops up, "Moonbeam. Hey. What are you...I thought you and Chad—"

"Whoa," she breathes, cutting me off, quickly closing the distance between us and grabbing my hands. "Your aura is..."

"All the colors of the rainbow?" I offer cutting back in.

But before I can say anything else, she shakes her head. "No...it's sad. Like black and gray."

I blink, my face going blank. I swallow as I look around wondering if this is some kind of joke. "You're kinda freaking me out."

She nods with a sympathetic smile. "Yeah, that happens a lot. But listen," she hooks an arm around mine, "You could use a soul cleansing. Come with me."

I'm shaking my head, but she doesn't let go, so I shuffle along next to her. "Uhh, where exactly are you proposing we scrub down my soul?"

"My room," she says cheerily.

My brows hit my forehead as the elevator doors open and we step inside. "What about Chad? Didn't you leave him for Scottie?"

She rolls her eyes. "My heart holds capacity for so much, Millie. I don't believe connected souls ever really leave each other—"

I laugh, and she stops talking. "Scottie have room-mates? Buncha gross surfers?"

Moon winks at me, all the bullshit aside. "Yeah. It'll take a couple of days to clear them out. In the meantime, Ajax left for his gig. He won't be back until tomorrow. Because he's got a hot little Gemini rising who's keeping him company."

I don't really know what to say and honestly this day has been a rollercoaster anyway. The doors close but she looks at me, one eyebrow raised.

So, I shrug. "Fuck it. I'm dying to see what I booked anyway."

"The universe provides," she purrs.

I'm smiling but the minute the elevator starts moving, she turns and stares at me before saying the most unex-pected shit ever.

"So, do they know you're crazy about them? Or do they think you guys are all still faking it?"

My face slowly meets Moon's, and I swear if I didn't like her before, I do now.

Unreal. She knew. And never ratted me out. My ex's ex is a real girl's girl.

Two hours later, Moon and I mini-barred, invited Eleanor up, and swam in the fucking infinity pool. Now we're lying on the floor, trying to cleanse my bad love luck with various crystals around me.

And I can't tell anyone it reminds me of my first beach day with the guys.

"I got this little beauty from a healer in Costa Rica,"

Moon says, holding up a little brown stone as Eleanor oohs and ahhs from her chair. "We had a wildly passionate affair, but then he got weird and wanted me to do some strange shit in a fishbowl—" My head pops up, eyes wide, before she gently guides it back down to the floor. "Don't move. Anyway, I bounced and then ended up in the VIP section of some music festival. That's where I met your Fuf. Anyway, that's my story. Eleanor, share yours."

I do move again, sitting up as Elle says, "Well, I met Crew in Vegas…"

"That's for another day," I say, interrupting, "Moon… my what?"

Moon laughs, looking at me like what she said is something that's common knowledge. "Your P.H. Or *Fuf*…it stands for placeholder. Ajax was holding space that wasn't his. He was your relationship placeholder. But you already know that."

"That part," Eleanor agrees, pointing at me with her chocolate-covered strawberry.

It was the first thing she ordered up on Chad's dime. Along with the Dom Pérignon she's refilling in her glass.

I half shrug. "Well, whoever this space belongs to should start making haste because I'm giving up on dating."

Eleanor groans, falling back against her chair dramatically. "Can we puhleasse talk it about now? I think you're cleansed…you're ready." She looks at Moonbeam with her brows raised. "Right? Tell her…" Moon waves her fucking hands around me before she nods.

"See?" Eleanor presses. "The resident aura magician knows her shit."

How is it that in this season of my life, I'm not the weird one?

"Fine," I snap, getting off the floor. "But there's not much to say. I took them to the waterfall like I planned. We had a great time. I came back, and then Chad tried to kiss me..." My face swings Moon's way for a moment. "Sorry about that... And then, all of a sudden, all I know is that they have their own room. And they're saying things like 'clean break.'"

Moon stands too, walking toward the kitchen—there's a full fucking kitchen. Fuck you, Chad. Still and again.

"We should make them a matcha," she offers with all the confidence in the world. "That'll unblock them. Then they can pick up what you're putting down, sister."

Is this getting stranger, or is it my imagination?

"Wait a fucking minute."

Eleanor's voice makes me jump. My head whips her way as she clamors to her feet, strawberries falling to the floor. She doesn't even bother to pick them up as she rushes toward me. "When did Chad try and kiss you?"

"Earlier. Right after the waterfall. It doesn't matter. I wanted to vomit...and then he started crying about Moonbeam. It was gross." My hand lifts in Moon's direction. "Again, no offense."

Eleanor's hands come to her hips. "Did the Tweedles see?"

I run my hands through my hair, turning my head to stare out at the ocean. "Yes. But they were fine... It's not that or the need for matcha. They don't need to pick up what I'm putting down. I think they did. That's the problem. They didn't want it. TJ all but said so."

Eleanor's bottom lip sticks out before she wraps her arms around me and gives me a tight hug.

"I'm sorry. I will never speak to them again for the rest of my life."

I laugh, letting her squeeze me.

"Shut up. They didn't do anything wrong. I'm just bummed." She lets me go as Moonbeam slides a glass filled with green liquid in front of me. But I keep talking. "All this time, I've been dating and dating, trying to find my place next to someone. I thought that's maybe why I've been so unlucky in love for so long. Because I wasn't supposed to be next to someone; I was meant to be between them."

I bring the glass up and take a drink as Elle tries to hide her smile because whatever I just put in my mouth is something...something I'll never drink again.

I'm about to ask what the fuck I just ingested when Moon sniffles. Whoa. Elle and I immediately turn our attention to Moonbeam.

She's crying, wiping her eyes.

And suddenly, I feel like such a dick saying all that stuff about Chad in front of her. My hands come to my chest.

"Moon, I'm so sorry."

She waves me off. "No. You have nothing to be sorry about. This is just so beautiful. When you hugged just now, Eleanor healed your aura. It's just such a testament to women." She raises her hands to articulate the point. "Women, you know! Women."

I know my mouth is hanging open as I smile. *Because Moonbeam, you know, Moonbeam.* I'm sad I'm only getting to know her now.

Eleanor looks at me, brushing invisible dust off her shoulder before she impersonates the medium lady from *Poltergeist.* "Your house is clean. You're welcome, bitch."

I laugh, for real. Deep and loud.

On second thought. Fuck boys. Who needs them when you have girlfriends.

tj

"Dude, what is taking so long?" Nate grumbles.

He's gonna be a bastard from tomorrow until he dies because we fucked up.

I shout through the bathroom door, "I told you I had business in here. I'll be out in a minute. You don't have to wait for me."

He bangs on the door again. "She already fucking hates us, and now you're going to drop a deuce before we leave? For real, Teej."

Fuck. I reach over and open the bathroom door and sweep my hand past my body, inviting him in, revealing what I've been doing for the last twenty minutes.

"What the fuck, TJ—" The rest of whatever he was going to say gets caught in his throat as he takes in the bathroom mirror.

It's littered with Post-it notes in the shape of a heart. Well, not yet, but I was working on it.

He looks back at me again, his voice quieter this time. "What are you doing, TJ?"

I sit back against the counter, crossing my arms.

"Well, since you're asking so politely." I lift a finger, pointing toward the two-dollar art installation. "This was going to be her Valentine's Day gift from me."

Nate chuckles. "Roses and chocolates were a no-go?"

I cock my head, being cocky. "Why you gotta be such a basic bitch, Nathan… It's like an affirmation wall. Just all the things I think make her special. I figured it still applied, even without us around."

He's silent. But Nate's a thinker. That's just him. So, I stay in my place and let him weigh out all the pros and cons, even though I already have.

After a couple of minutes, he takes a deep breath and says, "You should add the way she always gives the extra squeeze at the end of every hug."

I hand him a marker. "Or you could add it."

Nate takes it from my hand, peeling off a sticky note before he adds it to my half-shaped heart.

I peel one off too, writing the way her lip gloss always tastes good. He laughs, reading it.

"Dude, always. It's like the flavor never wears off her lips. It's a superpower."

Nate and I stand there in the bathroom, peeling sticky after sticky, filling up an entire heart before we take a step back and look at our creation.

But then he frowns, mirroring my expression.

"You think we'll ever get another shot?"

"Only if you believe in fate."

Which we don't. So, we're still fucked.

twenty-nine

. . .

"Happy Venereal's Day."

millie

I talked a lot of shit yesterday with the whole "Fuck boys, who need 'em" album I'm about to drop. But right now, walking back to my room after being up too late with Eleanor and Moonbeam, I could very much use a Nate piggyback ride.

I smile to myself, thinking about this morning and how Chad found me sleeping in his bed.

With Moonbeam.

God, the boys would love this story.

Nothing says full-circle revenge than finding the girl you proposed a threesome with, *in bed*, with the girl who broke up with you because of that proposition.

Plus, the fact that nothing happened. That we just jumped on the bed and sang Miley Cyrus songs all night is something he never has to know.

And that is the gift that keeps on giving.

I smile as I walk past the housekeepers who are parked just outside my room.

"Good morning," I offer with a smile, noticing an inordinate number of Post-it notes in the garbage can. Weird.

I pull up my key and open the door, but the minute it closes behind me, I am struck with the harsh reality that I'm alone.

No Tweedles.

On Valentine's Day.

My phone vibrates, so I swipe it open, seeing a text from Eleanor.

> Elle: Happy Venereal's Day.

> Elle: whoops autocorrect.

Why is that her default?

> Me: Wanna hear something funny? Chad caught me and Moon... in bed together.

> Elle: Well played, bitch. Tell me all about it at the pool this morning?

> Me: Pass. I'm going back to sleep. Wake me up when it's time to leave.

> Elle: K...but party's at 8.

> Me: No. For home tomorrow.

I know she's texting back a slew of ridiculous emojis and "you better come tonight" threats. But I don't care because all I want is my damn bed.

Which is exactly what I head for, kicking off my shoes and crawling in before grabbing TJ's pillow and inhaling.

Dammit. They already cleaned the room.

I drag it over my head and let sleep take me again. Tomorrow means home and freedom from the guys I can't stop thinking about.

tweedles

tj

Nate checks his phone with hope for the millionth time. I've been doing the same thing too, so I can't hate.

Come on, Smalls, just tell us you liked the mirror.

The beep at our door calls our attention as I look up to see Eleanor strolling in.

"How the fuck did you get a key—" I laugh, casually pointing to the door.

"It's seven forty-five," she offers, tossing Nate a package before doing the same to me. "Get dressed."

I sit up on my bed, turning off SportsCenter, and she smirks.

"Watching highlights of yourself again, TJ? There are better ways to cheer yourself up."

I scowl, rubbing my stomach over my shirt, as Nate puts his arms behind his head over on his bed, not touching the package.

"Why are you here, Elle? Shouldn't you be hanging with your future husband?" he grumbles.

She shrugs, not answering, circling her finger at the packages. "Open them."

Nate and I glance at each other before begrudgingly doing what she's insisting.

My forehead wrinkles, surprise written on my face as I pull out the contents. "Why are you giving me a watermelon Speedo?"

She crosses her arms as her eyes narrow. Uh-oh. Nate and I glance at each other again because we've seen this face before.

Eleanor's about to deliver a come-to-Jesus.

She huffs a laugh. "These are your costumes for tonight. For the Lovers Only party. The one you're supposed to be attending with my best friend."

Nate lets out a harsh breath and tosses his costume to the end of the bed.

"It's not happening."

"Nathan DeLuca," she barks.

But I agree with Nate, drawing her ire as I say, "We haven't heard from her all day. If we thought for a minute that girl had any interest in us showing up, you couldn't keep us away."

Eleanor throws her hands in the air. "I knew it. She was wrong." I frown, totally confused as she starts ranting and pointing between us. "Don't you look at me and act like you two don't know that you made the biggest mistake of your lives calling it early on this fake relationship. You do like her. This isn't a hit-and-quit homance."

I hold up a hand. "Whoa. She told you about us faking it?"

Eleanor rolls her eyes. "Of course, she told me. And *clean break*? Really, guys?"

"What were we supposed to do?" Nate levels back, sitting with his feet on the ground now. "Sit around and wait for her to be done with us? Fuck that, Eleanor. Remind us, is that what you did for Crew?"

Gotcha. She fucking bounced, too, before Crew could end it.

Eleanor grabs his costume, tossing it back at him. "Oh, boo-hoo. You're scared she'll reject you. That's what this is. But I've never seen any of you happier in all the time I've known all of you. How do you not see that? I know you get hit in the head for a living, but you can't actually be this obtuse."

"That means stupid," I say to Nate, being as sarcastic as possible as we both rise to our feet.

"Big risk equals big reward," she spits as we close in on her.

"Tell her that," Nate growls as I nod. "She's the one who friend-zoned us, not the other way around. She made sure to remind us we were fake."

Eleanor shakes her head, but Nate sighs, picking her up by the armpits, even as she protests, and walks her toward the door as I open it.

"Oh my god," she grinds out. "Actions speak louder than words. If you couldn't see how she felt about you after she planned that whole waterfall date, you don't deserve her anyway."

Eleanor's feet hit the ground as I shut the door with her still in the room.

Hold up. "Date?" I level. "That was just a thank-you."

"No, that was an offer. She's hooked on you two."

"What did you say?" Nate grinds, bending to make them eye to eye. "Repeat that."

A sly smile blooms over her face. "You two *are* dummies. Your girl likes you back. More than you deserve. The waterfall was her attempt to woo you into dating the girl, you fuck. She just doesn't have any game. It's like the blind leading the blind with you three."

Oh fuck. All this time. We've been in the right book on the wrong page. We're thinking she's got a clock set. And she's thinking we're here for a good time, not a long time.

Nate rises back to his full height, staring straight at me as the rest of what Eleanor says hangs like a challenge.

"So, now that you know, what are you going to do about it?"

thirty

. . .

"Nobody puts our baby in the corner."

millie

"I feel stupid," I complain as Crew pushes me forward through the doors of the Lovers Only hotel party. I wave my hand toward a couple dressed as Tweedle-Dee and Tweedle-Dum. "For real? This is an omen. Let me make a break for it."

He looks down at me, shaking his head and laughing. "You're nuts. It's all good. I told you they aren't coming. Plus, if I don't produce my Cleopatra's bestie, she said she wouldn't marry me."

"Whatever. Who knew Mark Antony was such a pushover. You've got a sword, for Christ's sake," I snark.

I know she sent him not because he's irresistible or even charming. But because Crew's a damn giant and part caveman. If I'd said no, he would've just thrown me over his shoulder and dragged me down here anyway.

He grins, making the fake sword clink against the metal shin guard things over his boot. "It's cool, right?"

251

I roll my eyes, giving in and laughing. *Freaking men.*

The deeper into the party we get, the more self-conscious I become. "I'm gonna kill her. My costume's a single now…this party is for the lovers."

He brushes me off. "You're fine. You match with anyone. Nobody'll know. If someone asks, just choose someone random and say, 'I'm with them.'"

I point to a Bert and Ernie. "Like them?"

Crew nods, ignoring my sarcasm. "Solid choice." He's grinning as he looks down at me, leading me toward the bar. "Who are you anyway? Marilyn Monroe?"

I smooth my hands over my dress, scowling. "You ill-mannered heathen. No, I'm Baby… You know, Jennifer Grey from *Dirty Dancing.*"

"Ohhh," he draws out as the bartender approaches, and I order. "That makes so much sense now."

I look around at the sea of Romeo and Juliets, most circa Leo and Claire, and a SpongeBob and Patrick. *I like the direction.* A chuckle bubbles out as two people walk by as Frank and Beans, the guy outfitted in a full hot dog. Mustard included.

What Crew said finally catches up to me, so I turn and look at him.

"Why does that make sense?"

His eyes narrow as he stares at the bar, his smile tight.

"Umm…" he answers as his lips pull to the side like he's trying not to smile.

"Crew…" I breathe out, my eyes growing wide. "Crew…" I say again, elongating his name as I lean closer to him. "What's going on?"

He looks at me, stealing my drink and downing it before he brings a heavy hand to my shoulder. "It makes sense for why Nate looks like a dude from the fifties. And

TJ's in a watermelon Speedo? Clever. That scene's funny when she's carrying it over that bridge. Also, this was not my idea."

My heart's beating out of my chest as I stare up at him because I'm having a fucking heart attack. I grip his bicep, my nails digging in as he says, "Ow," forcing him to look at me.

"You dirty liar. You said they weren't going to be here. But they are...aren't they?"

He winces, only nodding as his answer.

My head whips around, eyes scanning the crowd but coming up empty.

"Mills," Crew presses, bringing my face back to his.

"It's Miss Dwyer for you. You're dead to me, Matthews, and that hoochie you plan to marry is too."

He laughs, crossing his arms. "Don't be mad at me. All's fair in love and war... I love her, so that means I'm not going to war." I narrow my eyes at him, but he taps my nose. "This could be the start of the rest of your life."

"Shut up...is that above the door at your gym?" He laughs loudly, but I push him, even though he's unmovable. "I'm outta here. Tell Cleopatra to watch her back."

But as I start to leave, my phone vibrates, and it stops me in my tracks because the crowd's parted, and there they are.

My guys, looking ridiculous and adorable.

My brows draw together as I swipe open our group text.

shit you can only say in the dark

TJ: You look amazing, Baby.

He capitalized it, so he gets it.

> Nate: We fucked up.

I hear the gasp. My teeth find my lip, because yeah, you did. And also, me too.

> TJ: But we meant everything we said on the mirror.

What mirror? What did they say on the mirror? I look up, my face shifting between them in the distance, confused before I look back down and type.

> Me: What mirror?

Bubbles, and then they go away.

Nate and TJ look at each other, and they seem to be talking before a group of people crowd in front of me, so I look up at Crew.

"What did they do on a mirror?"

A vee forms between his eyes before it relaxes, and he nods. "You mean the Post-its on the bathroom mirror?"

"I don't know what you're talking about. I didn't see anything today..." My eyes get big. "The housekeepers cleaned the room. They never put the DND up."

My hand comes to my mouth as I look back at them before I text again.

> Me: Crew explained. The housekeepers took it all. I didn't see. What did it say?

Immediately, text after text populates, all with things they like about me from the way I remember obscure movie lines to how I also pet people's dogs. They're coming in so fast that I can't even read them before another shows up.

An airy laugh leaves me as I shake my head to make sure it's clear.

> Me: What does this all mean? Because you left and wanted a clean break. You don't date the girls you fuck. And I'm definitely the latter. So what does this mean?

> TJ: It was never fake.

> Nate: You've always been the real deal for us.

The music stops, kind of like my heart. And I feel myself nudged, so I look at Crew, who has a sly grin on his face as he leans against the bar.

You could hear a pin drop, but I'm still reeling until applause spreads out around the room. All the people in front of me begin to yell as the song from Dirty Dancing begins to play.

A nervous laugh pops from my chest as Crew, who's now shaking his head in the way he does when Nate and TJ are doing something insane, begins guiding me through the crowd.

People shift out of the way until finally, my eyes fall on something at the front I never thought I'd see.

TJ and Nate are standing in the center of the cleared dance floor.

Grins on their faces. Mischief in their eyes. TJ points right at me and yells, "We'll make fools of ourselves all damn day, girl, if it means you give us another shot."

The music kicks up louder, and I swear to god, they start doing the goddamn dance from the movie.

My hands immediately cover my mouth as I scream a laugh.

Oh. My. God.

They look insane. TJ in his Speedo, shirtless like a juicy snack, and Nate looking fine as hell in those black pants and dress shirt.

Nate glances over at Eleanor and Moonbeam, who are off to the side on the stage doing the moves and yelling directions. So I smack Crew's arm, making him look as he laughs with me.

There isn't a person at this party who isn't clapping and yelling for them. My guys. Dancing like lunatics. All for me.

They only dance for a few seconds, but it feels like the dreamiest lifetime. Except it keeps getting better.

Nate grins and gives me the Patrick Swayze come 'ere move as TJ bellows, "Nobody puts our baby in the corner."

I squeal as the crowd erupts, chanting do it over and over. Oh, I've always wanted to do this. They just get me.

The grin on my face stays, and I nod like I'm ready. Just like Jenny G.

And without any worry, I kick off my shoes and run, barreling toward them until I'm up in the air, suspended in the pose, held up by both of them.

Moon and Elle are jumping up and down on the stage, making me laugh too hard before I collapse. But I'm caught by my guys.

I'm set to the floor, TJ taking my hand and spinning me around before he pulls me flush to him, dancing with me slowly as Nate kisses the back of my head.

"I'm sorry," I breathe out. "I should've just been honest about how I felt for you guys."

"Same," TJ whispers, kissing my temple.

Nate's deep baritone encases me from behind. "But from now on, we're all retiring from the lies and revenge game."

I nod, pressing my lips to TJ's, saying, "Deal," before I spin around.

Nate grabs me, lifting me so we're eye to eye as he smiles back. "Hey, fake girlfriend. Gimme a real kiss."

My arms wrap around his neck before I feel TJ's hands on my waist, pawing at me. "Get off my girlfriend."

I giggle as Nate winks, keeping his voice low enough for only the three of us as I'm lowered back down to the ground.

"I don't want to be here. I want to be balls-deep inside our girl, making her come."

"One day without me and you're already malnourished?" I tease.

TJ lifts my hand, biting the side. "Feed us, Smalls. We're in desperate need of your pussy."

My hands come to their chests, acting like I'm holding them back. "And what do I get out of this new arrangement?"

TJ brings his finger to his chin, pretending to think before he says, "Hmmm, two very loyal boyfriends who will make it their mission to keep you wet and happy?"

Nate chuckles, adding, "And who make sure you know how fucking amazing you are every single day."

I take a very deep sigh, like what they're saying is torture to contemplate before I wink. "Add in some of those Valentine's heart candies from the bar and you've got yourself a deal."

I'm hoisted directly over Nate's shoulder as TJ procures the goods, and we literally walk off into the sunset.

My guys and me. Our own little pre-love story unfolding.

Maybe not the typical kind, but definitely the more fun version.

If someone were to ask me at the start of the week if I thought this was how my week would end, I could have never imagined something so wild and perfect.

But now...my answer is locked.

I'll take sex on the beach for a thousand, Alex.

epilogue

· · ·

"Two dirty Cupids."

millie

"Apologies, ma'am, but I show your room has already been checked in."

My hands slap the counter as I stare at the front desk person. This is not happening again. What are the odds?

"Stop it. This is a joke." I smile, waiting for the punchline. "That's impossible. Tell me you're lying."

One year ago today. In this very hotel. I went from the worst moment of my life to the two best. And now I'm back at the Four Seasons to surprise said boyfriends with a Valentine's Day they won't forget.

I even got here a day early, so they didn't know I was up to something.

"Can you check again?" I press.

The hotel clerk nods, then winces. "I'll need to call my manager."

I suddenly hear my name being called, so my head

shifts around, recognition setting in. Especially the minute my eyes land on who it is.

"Moonbeam?"

She rushes me, wrapping me in her signature full-body hug, then pulls away with her hands on my shoulders before one of them drops to her stomach.

Oh my god. I haven't seen or heard from her in true Moon style since we left last year.

"A baby," I rush out. "You're having a baby."

She laughs, nodding, making her stomach jump and a long crystal hanging from one of her necklaces fall to the side.

"We are. Fate is so unexpected. Miss one flight and find the love of your life."

That must be the "how I met your father" version.

Speaking of the devil, he strolls up, looking exactly how I remember, and throws an arm over her shoulder.

"Wow. Mickie, right?" I don't correct him. Fair's fair. He looks lovingly to Moon. "Babe, we gotta get going. That tantric yoga retreat can't start itself."

I chuckle. "I mean, they're pros at waiting though, right?"

Nobody laughs, so I smirk and hug her one more time before she walks away.

"Wow," I breathe out, turning back around to the clerk.

But as I do, my heart rate hits an all-new high. The manager standing in front of me is another blast from the past.

"Paul."

The same guy from last year smirks at me, sliding a key across the counter.

"It looks as if this time, a key was left for you. Enjoy

your stay, Miss Dwyer. And thank you for the five-star review, naming me."

"You're welcome."

My mouth opens and closes because the number of butterflies cycloning in my tummy makes me wonder if they'll escape. I don't know how fast I turn, but all I hear behind me is, "It's okay. We'll have your luggage delivered."

Oh yeah, my bags. Fuck them.

Nothing stops my stride to the elevator and even down the hall. I'm so antsy that I could die. Because I know exactly who's behind this.

My two favorite Tweedles. The loves of my life.

The moment I get to the room, I take a deep breath before inserting the card and opening the oversized door.

We're in one of those rich rooms. They upgraded us.

But I don't get to admire it because a laugh instantly bursts from me, and I'm struck with sheer joy.

My guys are standing in the center of the room. Vases upon vases of pink and red roses are scattered around. There are even petals on the floor.

With "Let's Get It On" by Marvin Gaye playing in the background.

And they're clad in white Speedos, red bow ties...and angel wings.

Like two dirty Cupids.

TJ's holding a tiny bow and arrow while Nate strums an equally tiny harp.

My hands cover my mouth as TJ lets the arrow go with a little ping sound, and they both say, "Surprise."

A year ago, I flew all the way to Hawaii to lick my wounds. To get over an ex and find myself again. But what I left with was even better than I planned.

"I can't believe you out-surprised my surprise."

Nate shrugs, strumming his little harp again. "Baby, that's what we do...we keep you on your toes."

TJ cuts in. "We remind you that you're special."

"That we can't live without you," Nate adds.

They're doing that thing...verbally tag teaming me as they stalk toward me.

"Because you're our reason."

"The only one we want...forever."

TJ stops in front of me, his hand cradling my face. "I love you, Smalls."

I smile, kissing him before Nate whispers in my ear, "But I love you more."

God, I hope some things never change.

My hands come to their chests, holding them in place.

"Here's the play. First one to catch me gets to make me come. Loser licks it off my thighs."

Thank you for reading Millie and her guys.
If you'd like to see who catches her first,
join my newsletter.

SMUTTY ROMANTIC COMEDIES

PREP SCHOOL BOOKS

ROMEO AND JULIET RETELLING (HEA)

BDSM MAFIA BOOKS

acknowledgments

What a wild ride.

I owe so many thank you's to so many people. But let me start with those who have shown up for me time after time and always been by my side.

To my readers: We are besties. I know that. You know that. I'm eternally grateful for all your support.

Sandy—I literally couldn't do this without out.

You too Sarah! I love you endlessly and can't wait to do Vegas again with you.

My ride-or-die team: (a different) Sarah, Kelsey, and Serena. You know I'd be completely lost without you. I legit love you so so much. #soulmates

Brielle, twin…where have you been? You hold down PR and make the game look easy.

KATIE…all caps because to me, you're everything, and without you, I'd cry and rock in a corner. You make me the best version of myself. And I love you so much.

And my friends, who I don't need to name because my love for them isn't about clout. lol. Thanks for cheering me on. Always believing in me. Finding me the perfect songs. Listening to the jokes that never make the cut and being ready for whatever comes out of my mouth!

To everyone above, thank you for always telling me the truth. It's a priceless gift in this industry.

Now, the best for last: **Anthony, Georgia, Charlie, and Hayes.**

They tell me their proud of me every day. They rearrange work schedules and never complain when I have to skip out on something. They love me unconditionally.

And I love them the same.

about the author

#1 Amazon and USA TODAY Bestselling Author, Trilina Pucci, loves cupcakes and bourbon.

When she isn't writing steamy love stories, she can be found devouring Netflix with her husband, Anthony, and their three kiddos. Pucci's journey into writing started impulsively. She wanted to check off a box on her bucket list, but what began as wish fulfillment has become incredibly fulfilling. Now she can't see her life without her characters, her readers, and this amazing indie community.

She's known for being a trope-defier, writing outside the box and creating fictional worlds her readers never want to leave. With every book and each character, she's committed to writing book boyfriends worth binging and smut worth savoring.

Connect with Trilina and stay up to date.

Made in United States
North Haven, CT
08 July 2024

54549579R00154